'Thou shalt not suff

'She did call upon her master for aid. And then one of her curs'd familiars did come creeping to her.'

It had been a rat. Brown, hair matted with dust, sneaking out from behind some old ale kegs in the furthest corner of the cellar. Liza had seen it first. Daniel had killed it.

'In her struggles to escape our rightful questioning the witch did throw herself against the walls and did injure herself with her own foolishness.'

There always had to be some kind of explanation slipped in somewhere to explain the fact that many of those interrogated by Monk and his team showed signs of some injuries.

The truth was generally different . . .

Also by James Darke in Sphere Books:

THE WITCHES 1: THE PRISONER
THE WITCHES 3: THE TORTURE

The Witches: Book 2
The Trial

JAMES DARKE

SPHERE BOOKS LIMITED
30–32 Gray's Inn Road, London WC1X 8JL

First published in Great Britain by
Sphere Books Limited 1983

Reprinted 1983

TRADE
MARK

Set in 11½/12½ Compugraphic Paladium

Printed and bound in Great Britain by
Cox & Wyman Ltd, Reading

Listen, you got the kind of eyes that do more than see and you're everything I'm dreamin' of. This is with all of my heart for Liz, who's a real dead ringer for love.

'One of the darker pages in our nation's chequered history is in the middle part of the seventeenth century when hundreds of innocent folk were hounded to their miserable and tortured ends by the arts of that most evil breed of men, the witchfinders. Men such as Matthew Hopkins and Robert Monk deserve only the eternal flames of Hell for their wicked works.'

From: 'The True Facts In The Matter Of The Persecution Of Witchcraft And Daemonologie' by Father Damien Murray, Published by The Circle Press of Bloomsbury, 1828.

'Thou shalt not suffer a witch to live.' Exodus, Chapter 21, Verse 18.

CHAPTER ONE

The parchment was speckled with small, irregular brown spots of blood. Dried blood.

And a corner of it was scorched where one of the hot irons had been placed carelessly upon it, the edge of the paper curling from the heat of the nearby brazier. For the magistrates it was important that the confession should be made out in a neat, clerkly hand, without errors and without any blemish. With a space at the bottom corner of the final page where the witch could scrawl her mark, the quill guided between her shaking fingers, carefully avoiding the broken ends of her jagged, torn nails.

A triple candelabrum stood at one side of the large oak table, casting a steady, golden light across the piles of paper. The glass well of ink and the horn beaker containing several quills. A fire crackled in a corner of the tavern room, flames licking merrily at the hewn logs. Outside the shutters a wind was rising, rattling the hinges, making the smoke dance in the hearth.

A long cheval mirror, one corner starred as if something had been flung against it, was set by a bureau. The man at the table glanced up and saw himself reflected in it. Smiling at his own image, raising his right hand and stroking at the trim beard. Turning his head from side to side to try and decide whether he should ask for a visit from the local barber. Deciding that it would wait.

Picking up the confession once more and going through it, making several small alterations. It still lacked a half hour or so until he retired and then the papers could go out to be copied.

And then . . .?

He glanced to the further side of the chamber, where a massive four-poster bed held a promise of comfort to come later. The curtains were drawn against the draughts from the chimney and the ill-fitting door. On the chair at the foot of the bed lay a woman's gown, crumpled and travel-stained. It was of pale green silk, edged with muddied lace. On the floor was a pair of shoes, in matching silk, their heels trodden down and worn.

The man smiled.

Going back once more to the beginning of the document, reading it carefully through. Letting his mind run back to the events that were covered in the parchment.

It had been less than a week since he and his party had returned from Normandy. Yet, already there was a call on his services from a magistrate not far from Dover. Suspicion of a coven, led by a tall man. A stranger. Who had most conveniently disappeared, leaving only his poor lackbrain disciples.

For Robert Monk, Witchfinder, they were all grist to his gold-hungry mill.

'And please your lordships, this is a true and sworn account of the questioning of the alleged witch,

Charlotte Ellison. Carried out in the hamlet of Cold Easter in the County of Kent. By Robert Monk, Witchfinder. With the assistance of Daniel Mendoza and Abraham Mendoza.'

The third of the brothers dead long months back. Killed by . . . His eyes turning again to the bed with its secret behind the long drapes.

Turning back to the papers, carrying on reading them out to himself in a quiet, grey voice.

'The woman Liza Hall was of great aid in questioning the witch Mistress Ellison and did help much in testing her for the marks of her master.'

Monk stopped for a moment, a half-smile curling about his narrow lips at the memory. Charlotte Ellison had been a widow, not ill-favoured. Most of the harridans who were brought to the attention of the witchfinders were elderly and filthy. Lacking interest in their own appearances, often covered in more lice than clothes, mostly well past their fiftieth year.

Mistress Ellison could have been only a little past forty.

'The teats where the woman suckled her familiars were most cunningly concealed, as would be looked for in one who was the instrument of Satan himself. Only with the most rigorous examination could they be discovered.'

It was surprising how frequently they found the little blemishes and wrinkles among the folds of flesh around the sexual organs and between the cleft of the buttocks. Daniel Mendoza was particularly skilled at the latter. Probing and spreading with his strong, brutal hands.

It took precious little effort for Monk to recall the exact details of the examination. And the recollection brought a familiar and pleasurable tightness to the front of his well-cut breeches.

The village of Cold Easter stood in a shallow valley about eighteen miles from the sea. Not a part of the land where there had been many instances of wizardry and deviltry, but the name of Monk was a sure remedy for that. Any lonely woman who dealt in herbs and charms was fair game for his bow. And his arrows rarely missed their marks.

The local squire, Alexander Hewer, was a tall, lean man, whose face showed all too clearly his affection for good ale. He was more than happy to allow Robert Monk and his entourage to stay at the small manor house on the eastern side of the hamlet. And to use an abandoned cellar for their interrogation.

A low room, with vaulted ceiling, and a range of square, barred windows. A hearth with a chimney that had smoked abominably until one of the Mendozas had arranged for it to be swept.

For a moment the eyes of Robert Monk became hooded. Recalling the way that he had found the third of the gipsy brothers.

'Benjamin.'

Lying in the yard of an inn, dead in the pallid light of the moon. Face smashed in from a kick, arms and legs twitching uncontrollably as the lines went down 'twixt limbs and brain. Blood inching from the open mouth. The cobbled yard filled with the stench of dying as the man's bladder and bowels opened uncontrollably.

'Benjamin Mendoza,' whispered Monk. His fingers gripping the edge of the table so that the knuckles whitened and seemed like to burst through the taut skin. And he breathed another name.

'Ferris. John Ferris. One day, Ferris, that debt shall be paid. Though the price I have taken already . . .' The words faded away into the stillness of the room. Silence broken only by the crumbling of the burned wood into grey ash.

'At first the woman Ellison did protest most strongly that she had no knowledge of the Evil One. But upon the discovery of the marks she did succumb to our entreaties and did confess her wickedness. Also naming others who shall soon be questioned.'

The search for the marks was always a matter of great pleasure for Liza Hall. She was a woman edging into mid-age, large-built, with the coarse manners and features of a privy-cleaner. She habitually smoked a clay pipe and would spit and curse harder than most men. And would also be quick to knock down anyone who crossed her with a mighty buffet of the fist.

And she was also quick to snatch what chances came her way for sexual pleasure. Regardless of the gender of her victim or lover.

Charlotte Ellison had been stripped naked. That came first. Always. It had been the first lesson that Monk had learned from his teacher, the Witchfinder-General himself, Matthew Hopkins. Strip the accused and she, or he, will lose all shreds of dignity.

They had walked her for a while. Round and round the chamber, past the fire. One of the brothers holding her by one arm, the other Mendoza gripping her by the other wrist. Keeping her moving for two long hours. She had wept and pleaded for mercy. Begged them to let her rest. Asked for water or food.

'She did call upon her master for aid. And then one of her curs'd familiars did come creeping to her.'

It had been a rat. Brown, hair matted with dust, sneaking out from behind some old ale kegs in the furthest corner of the cellar. Liza had seen it first.

'Fuckin' rat, lads,' she'd screamed, making them drop Mistress Ellison to the stone flags.

Daniel had killed it. Taking a slim-bladed dagger from his leather belt and hurling it underarm with lethal accuracy, bowling it over so that it shrieked like a human child. Then stamping on it with his iron-heeled boots. Pulping it into the floor.

'In her struggles to escape our rightful questioning the witch did throw herself against the walls and did injure herself with her own foolishness.'

There always had to be some kind of an explanation slipped in somewhere to explain the fact that many of those interrogated by Monk and his team showed signs of some injuries.

The truth was generally different.

Monk could visualise the woman. Body stretched out on the chipped table, arms straining against the rough cords that bit into the soft skin of her wrists. Ankles tethered to the opposite corners. Like a tortured letter 'X', her breasts firm and pointing to the ceiling. Face blank with terror and shock. Spittle dribbled from the sagging mouth and she was whimpering, softly, like a whipped puppy.

Liza Hall had been looking for the marks. Using a

steel bodkin with a wooden handle, probing at the prisoner's flesh. Pricking her again and again. Watching each tiny ruby as it blossomed on the skin. It was common knowledge that a witch suckled her familiars and that the places where she did this were immune to all feeling. Once those places were found you had the witch as good as convicted.

'Not on her bubbies, Master Monk. I have pricked them well. Even run the needle through and through each nipple.'

That was when they had gagged Charlotte Ellison. Abraham holding her head still, clamping fingers into the angle of her jaw, gripping her nostrils with the other hand so that she could scarcely breathe. While Daniel Mendoza jammed a hank of rag into the woman's mouth, knotting it in place with a length of rough hemp.

Liza Hall had burrowed between the witch's spread thighs, parting them and probing among the matted pubic hair. Complaining she couldn't see well enough. Prompting Daniel to bring a smoking torch from its sconce and thrust it against Charlotte Ellison's thighs. The hair sizzled and burned, making Liza Hall clap her hands with delight. Shouting she could now see well enough. The witch had fainted away and the room was filled with the stink of scorched flesh.

'In the cleft that lies between her frontal opening and her rear orifice did we discover a pair of teats, ill-matched. Upon further questions the accused did own to us that this was truly where she did give suck to her familiars. She named them as "Rareben", being a spotted lion of a size no greater than the hand of a child. And "Conake", being a white newt which she did order to creep at night into the nostrils of her enemies to addle their pates so that they knew not whether they stood upon head or toes.'

Monk smiled at the familiars. It was surprising what imagination some of these wicked women showed when giving names to their creatures. And always the local gentry liked such information. Near as much as they liked sometimes being allowed to watch as the questioning took place.

Once they'd found the small blemishes in her skin, Mistress Ellison had been eager to help them.

Liza had called out in triumph. 'I have 'em! I have 'em clear.'

Monk had walked across the room, hearing his own boot-heels clicking on the stone. The only sound apart from the rasping, laboured breathing of the helpless prisoner on the table. He had stooped, managing to control his own rising lust at her exposed sex. The glittering redness between the parted lips where Liza had used her bodkin.

'There,' she'd hissed. Poking again. 'See how she cries not out when I touch them lumps.'

'It be time for your meal, Master Monk,' Daniel Mendoza had muttered at that juncture. 'Leave me and Abe and Liza with this sluttish whore. Come again in an hour and the whole tale shall be set out for you, pretty as a trout on a silver platter.'

He had left them, tugging the heavy door closed behind him. Seeing out of the corner of his eye that Abe Mendoza could hardly wait for him to be gone. Already unlacing his breeches and pulling out his swollen member.

The food had been poor, though Master Hewer had clearly tried hard. A brace of rabbits and a haunch of venison that had been hung overlong. With some buttered parsnips and salt cabbage. The bread was fresh and tasty and there could be no complaints about the quality or the quantity of the ale served.

Hewer had mentioned that perhaps Master Monk might be contributing something towards the lodgings of his party. The Witchfinder had stood at that, reaching his right hand for the hilt of his sword. 'Twenty shillings a day for me, Sir. The same for my people. And the same yet again for every witch I uncover and prove. The woman will give us names, Sir. Names a'plenty. Already the reckoning stands at five golden pounds. And it is the custom among the villages I serve to offer a collection for the witchfinder if his work is well done.'

'It is a costly business, Master Monk,' insisted the magistrate.

'It is more costly if a warlock sets a murrain to your crops. Your cattle. Your health.'

'But could we not think of less?'

Monk smiled at the skinny landowner. Knowing from the tone of the man's voice that he had him in the palm of his hand. 'I shall be off to the north once more in a week or so, Sir. To my lands of Hertford and Essex where I am best known. So the debt is likely to be no more than five and twenty guineas.'

'That is . . .'

Monk interrupted him. 'I have found, as has my dear comrade Matthew Hopkins, that there are occasions that men protest our work. Question our charges. It has been tested and found that such men are oft'times in league with those very witches they seek to protect. Such men have been swum and found to be devoid of innocence. Is my meaning clear, Master Hewer?'

Secure in his chamber, Monk chuckled. His meaning had been very clear. So clear that Hewer had immediately made an extra contribution to the expenses of the witchfinding of ten more guineas.

Behind the curtains on the bed, he heard the rustle of movement. Reading through the confessions of the women never failed to rouse Monk, as he recalled every vicious moment. Perhaps he could leave the rest of the details until the morrow . . .?

But on the morrow he wished to be on and away to the north. Across the Thames. After the bitter experiences with the tall Captain Ferris, it was as well not to linger overlong in any one place.

Yet the great War still raged across the land. He knew that Ferris was a deserter from the Parliamentary forces. Injured in an accident nearly a year ago. A fall with a horse. It had shattered the bones of his left elbow. All of this Monk had learned over the months that he had spent with the others across the brimming grey-green waters in Normandy.

It had been tempting to stay over there in France, safe from the bloody-eyed vengeance of Ferris. But they had little love of the English, and even less interest in his claims to be able to seek out and destroy witches.

So they had set sail for England as the first gales of early September buffeted their frail barque. Hoping to earn enough before winter set its teeth in the throat of the land and the peasants lost interest in any sport but that of living. Living and partly living. Existing.

Monk shook his head. It was still full early and the warm body in the bed would wait a while longer for him. He picked up the parchment once more and started to read it again.

'The woman did also tell us of her companions in wickedness. Those names are herewith appended and shall be all rightly investigated.'

One had hung herself from a low beam in her miserable hovel before they even got to her. But Monk had claimed that this was a clear proof of her evil and had demanded – and received – the money due on her.

'Their coven did swear to take their vengeful ways against all in Cold Easter in the County of Kent. And in the surrounding hamlets of Danehill, Lower Norman and Upper Norman, Longholm Down, Garnett Trenthide and Albans Forkhill. The list of their strategems and devices are attached to this document with a full confession of what was done.'

When he had returned to the cellar, Charlotte Ellison had slipped away into a merciful and brief dark unconsciousness. Daniel Mendoza was sitting on the table, idly flicking at her nipples with his forefinger, amusing himself at the way they became erect and then subsided once more. Liza Hall was swigging ale from a horn beaker, squatting inelegantly in the straw against an empty barrel. Grinning at Abraham Mendoza who was hanging on the bars and pulling himself up so that he could look out over the darkening land.

'Clean her up,' snapped Monk, pointing with his gloved hand at where the helpless woman's thighs showed unmistakable evidence of the way that she had been used in his absence.

'She told us all, Master Monk,' giggled Liza, belching, putting a beefy hand to her mouth in a mock apology.

'Names?'

'Aye.'

'Places?'

'Aye.'

'Many?'

Mendoza laughed. 'More than enough for these yokels.'

'Is it ready for me to write down, Daniel?' asked Monk.

'Aye, I warrant it is, Master. She gave us goodly sport.'

'And me,' belched Liza Hall, dropping the mug on the stones so that it shattered into a hundred shards of horn.

'In conclusion,' he read, 'it is a matter with no doubt attaching that the woman is a witch. A witch admitted and sworn. With her demons listed clear and all manner of her evils confessed. It can be no argument that she is right worthy of suffering the ultimate penalty that the law of the land prescribes.'

There was a goblet of pewter at Monk's elbow and he picked it up, sipping thoughtfully. The claret was near finished, tasting flat to his tongue. He yawned, feeling that it was rightly the time for joining the wench in the four-poster. The fate of Mistress Charlotte Ellison was no longer of any concern to him.

Squire Hewer would see that the final 'i' was dotted and the last 't' crossed. Within the week the mewling shrew would be dead.

'And serve her right,' he sighed.

Glancing over the last lines of the sworn deposition, simply bearing his name and the titles that he had assumed to aid his business. A business that had gone exceedingly well, bearing ripe fruit.

As the land suffered beneath the fighting of King and Parliament, fear rode abroad on a nag with eyes of fire and teeth of flame. Every man was a'feared of his neighbour and betrayal lurked in the shadows of every penny alehouse. It was time for men like Robert Monk to flourish, dealing in treachery and lies. The organisation of law and order tottered throughout the country and many regions depended solely on the word of the local lord, much as it had hundreds of years back.

Robert Monk signed his name with a flourish, adding the date. The eighth day of the month of September in the year of Our Lord, Sixteen hundred and forty-five.

It was done.

Done well.

He stretched, standing and walking, light-footed, tugging the curtains slowly open. Looking at the naked woman who waited for him, smiling down at her. But as he moved the shadow of the curtain dropped between them and he drew back for a moment.

Unbidden, the face of a man swam before his eyes. And again his lips shaped the name.

'John Ferris.'

By a trick of the sinking firelight it seemed as if the woman echoed the name.

CHAPTER TWO

The elbow was paining him more than he had thought it would.

The surgeon who had attended to him had agreed with the judgement of John's father. Both doctors feeling that the injury was severe, with the joint swollen and fragments of splintered bone in the elbow likely to cause further trouble in later years.

Monk was wrong in judging John Ferris to be marked as a deserter. He had been discharged as being too severely injured to continue to serve the Parliament. He had even been granted the munificent pension of one shilling and four pence a week for his pains.

He reined in his horse, the ill-tempered, raw-boned bay mare, Morgana. Looking across the rolling green land, sniffing and tasting a small rain riding on the back of the easterly wind. The trees in the valleys ahead of him were already beginning to lose their colours, slipping into the duller browns of autumn. He sniffed again, tasting something else in the air.

'Smoke. A fire, and a big one,' he decided.

A soldier who had fought his way through some of the most cruel battles of the War recognised that smell. Almost as well as he would recognise the bitter-sweet scent of rotting flesh. The corruption of all things. If John Ferris closed his eyes he could easily see the expanded bellies of the eyeless corpses that decorated the fields of bloody carnage.

His hand dropped automatically to the ball-butt of his silver-chased pistol. A pretty weapon with a miquelet lock, made and signed by Ripoll of Catalonia. An expensive firearm for a poor invalided Captain. But in his mind he saw the dead man. A Cavalier, lying in the cold bracken of Marston Moor. Lace at collar and cuffs, smeared with blood and mud and horse-dung. A fine surcoat of maroon velvet, hat to match, its feather draggled and drooping in the earth. There was a broken rapier clutched in the man's white fingers and the Spanish pistol hidden in his sash.

Ferris had guessed that the man had been both officer and gentleman. His worth as he had ridden out on that doomed moor could not have been less than a hundred guineas in clothes and arms. And it had all been snatched away by a tuppenny butcher's knife, its hilt still protruding from the red-lipped wound in the neck.

Ferris had taken the pistol.

Still had it.

With practice he had managed to become a fair shot with the gun, though he lacked skill with a musket. His few attempts since his accident on the mare had been even less successful, as he found it hard to steady a heavy weapon with his left arm.

But he was good with a sword. Ferris was a big man, topping six feet by a full inch, his fourteen stone evenly distributed in muscle about him. His hair was black and thick, curling just beyond his collar. The eyes were grey, like the sky in winter when a storm threatens.

He was twenty-three years old.

A time in a young man's life when he should be seeking happiness and fulfilment.

All John Ferris wanted was revenge. As savage a vengeance as the Lord would permit him.

Against the monster, Robert Monk. Self-styled Witchfinder.

The smell of smoke came stronger as he heeled Morgana onwards. Making a steady pace towards the hamlet he had been told lay in a shallow valley three miles further on. Food would be welcome and some good ale. The journey up from the coast had been tiring, after the most malign crossing of the Channel he had ever known. The local sailors and fishermen had said it was such a storm that it surely heralded some great catastrophe. The death of a great King or even the birth of a new Anti-Christ.

It was not long before Ferris was able to make out a thin column of grey smoke, angling away from behind a clump of huge sycamores. And there was the tip of a church tower. It must be the hamlet that he was seeking.

Cold Easter.

The rain came in flurries, making him dip his head, hanging on to his wide-brimmed hat. Tugging it forwards to try and protect his face from the wet. The track wound among trees, that dripped as he passed. Ferris saw not a single living soul on the road and he wondered at the quiet. It could not be a feast day, or a fair.

The smoke grew thicker and he could now see that it came from the centre of the village.

As he turned a corner beyond a tiny, wattled hovel, he saw what was a'foot in Cold Easter that dull September morning.

And his heart quickened at the sight because he guessed that behind the dreadful scene lay the fell hand of Robert Monk.

Monk. The villain who had been responsible for the slaughtering of John's parents. And for the abduction of the girl who was closest to his heart. Sweet Mary Villers.

A middle-aged woman was being dragged around the village green on a hurdle. Spread-eagled and naked, her body smeared with mud and excrement and rotting vegetables. It was almost impossible to see her face, as it was covered in crusted blood, fresh crimson trickling from her nose and from the torn corners of her mouth.

A plodding horse drew the hurdle around, and Ferris saw why the houses and the country all about had been so deserted.

And the smoke . . .

It came from a great fire that was already burning brightly against a huge stake. But the men who had built it had taken care that there was still room for the victim to be attached. A way had been left open, so that the fire burned only on three sides of the stake.

Watching were fully two hundred men and women and children, mostly in silence. Some mocked the helpless woman as she was dragged by. A man, here and there, stepped from the front row and spat at her. And some of the women threw kitchen refuse and rubbish at the naked body.

As far as John could see, the woman was unconscious. Or had fainted. Which could have been a mercy.

He reined in the mare, snatching hard to control the iron-mouthed horse. Normally a stranger would have been a source of much interest in a small, isolated community, yet not a head turned for more than a second or two to gaze at him. The woman and the fire were of infinitely greater interest.

Someone called from beyond the fire and two men came scurrying out, carrying jugs of fat that they threw on the flames, making them sing and soar. John, from the height of the saddle, could see that the leader of the festivities was a tall, skinny man, dressed in a suit of good broadcloth of vastly better cut than anything anyone else there was dressed in.

'Bring the witch to the fire!' he shouted, voice thin and reedy.

The word 'witch' confirmed Ferris's suspicions. He had pursued Monk and his band over to France, but had lost track of them there. Nobody seemed to know aught of a man who could seek out witches. The Normandy peasants were a sturdy, close-mouthed folk, who disliked any stranger and mistrusted the English.

It had taken weeks before a chance conversation

in an inn had given him the clue that Monk was bound once more for the shores of England. And again he had missed him by scant hours, having to wait three days before the weather had abated sufficiently for him to hire a crossing on a fishing smack from Calais for himself and Morgana. Then on the road once more, following the neat, clerkly man in grey. The two gipsies, built like wrestlers. The harridan who smoked a clay pipe.

And the young woman with long hair as gold as summer corn, as virtuous as any virgin nun.

'Mary,' he said, unaware that he had even spoken out loud.

But nobody noticed or cared.

Men rushed eagerly to carry out the orders of their local lord, cutting the woman free and dragging her, willy-nilly, at a stumbling run, towards the fire. Only then did she seem to recover consciousness, head turning, eyes wildly seeking mercy.

'Help me! Help me, good neighbours. I am most wronged!!! Heeeeeeelp!'

'Get Beelzebub to aid you, beldame,' shouted a man near Ferris, wearing a blood-stained apron. Gripping a slaughterer's poleaxe in his right fist.

'Aye, let Satan rescue you from the fires,' added another.

The tall man waved a long cane, studded with silver at its top end. Urging speed. The fire was lapping eagerly at the stake, making it hard for them to drag the woman to it.

'It burns, Master Hewer,' bellowed one of the half dozen who had laid hands on the prisoner.

'Spare me. I am wronged. Spare me.'

Ferris watched, face unmoving, at the last scenes of the ritual killing. Watched as the one called Hewer stepped in, cane raised, and brought it down upon the side of the woman's face, breaking her jaw with a sickly crack. Hitting her twice more while the others held her. So that she slumped between them, silent.

'Thus do we deal with witches here in the good land of Kent,' he proclaimed proudly.

John watched him carefully, marking him down as a man who might merit some conversation a while later in the day.

'To the flames with her!'

'It be too hot, Master.'

'What?'

'Fire consumes stake.'

'Damnation and bloody perdition!!'

Ferris guarded a half-smile. There was a certain irony in watching these gullible bumpkins struggling to tie an unconscious woman to a stake and burn her. And yet allowing the stake to catch flame too early for their ends.

'Then throw her in. Keep her in the fire with staffs should she try and crawl free!'

And so they did.

Heaving the naked body as far into the crackling flames as they were able, giving out with a great cheer, as though one of them had captured the greasy pig at the Bartholomew's Fair.

John Ferris had never in his life heard a scream to match it.

He recalled that the Ferris family servant, Joshua Lightlantern, had once lit a great bonfire in the back garden of their neat Hertford cottage. Not knowing that a family of hedgepigs had taken refuge in the pile of bracken. Once the torch was applied to the heap of dry brush, the squealing began. John had only been a stripling, barely ten years old, but he could still recall the horror of that noise. The bristly little creatures bursting from the flames, their spines smoking and burning, making this painfully human sound. Old Joshua had recoiled from them, finally summoning the nerve to take his great fork and stick it through the hedgehog family, one after the other.

But that noise was nothing compared with this banshee wail.

The chatter of the cheerful mob was stilled in total shock. Faces turned away and mothers covered the ears of their young. Squire Hewer averted his eyes, looking along the rows of villagers. His gaze brushing past the tall man on the horse. Returning to him. Then passing on.

Charlotte Ellison was trying to crawl from the torment of the fire, scrabbling on blistered hands and knees, mouth open in a rictus of purest agony. The hair was burned away to a smouldering stubble and the eyebrows had disappeared into smudges of ash.

'Push 'er back in!' yelled someone, and the cry was taken up by the rest of the village.

While Ferris watched unmoving, for it was none of his concern and to try and save the woman would have only brought his own death, Hewer called to a couple of the men to get poles.

'Back to the flames with the witch!' he shrieked, his own shout almost lost beneath the pitiful screaming.

It took five grown men, using all their strength, pushing and heaving at the wretched woman, before they could push her back into the inferno. One of the sharp stakes caught her in the face, plucking an eye from its socket as neatly as a surgeon. It hung from her face, spinning and dangling, like an obscene bauble.

And the scream went on.

Even when they had her on her back among the highest flames, the noise did not abate.

Only when one of the men risked his own person, stepping in so close that his breeches began to scorch, using his staff as a club, did the persecutors manage to quiet the condemned woman. Beating at the blackened skull, until blood showed, smudged among the ashes.

Finally, she lay still.

Silent and still.

And the crowd began to drift away, some of the children remaining behind, ignoring the light drizzle that was beginning to fall, hissing among the glowing ashes. Ferris heeled Morgana onwards, sliding from her saddle, loosening the girths. There was a tumbledown alehouse in Cold Easter, and he went in, buying himself a pint of ale and a chunk of stale bread and some waxen cheese. Ignoring the attempts of the balding man behind the table to draw him into conversation. Moving out again as soon as he could, trying to find a spot where the stench of roasting flesh was less strong, and where the crackling of fat among the flames was less intrusive.

He sat down in a quiet corner, protected by the overhanging thatch of a long tithe barn, gnawing at the bread, draining the beaker of ale. Aware that the local squire was watching him from the furthest edge of the village green.

Was approaching him.

'Good day, Sirrah. Strangers are rare in Cold Easter. I am Squire Alexander Hewer, magistrate of this community and of the lands about.'

'Good day to you.'

'You are a stranger.'

'Aye.'

Hewer was poised awkwardly above him, hovering, his gawky limbs seeming disjointed as though they were made from a variety of broom-handles.

'Might I know your name, Sirrah?'

Ferris finished the drink, standing so suddenly that Hewer was forced to take a rapid step backwards. His face showing his alarm as he realised how tall Ferris was. His nervous eyes flicking to the silver butt of the pistol, and the worn hilt of the sword.

'The woman you burned, Magistrate?'

'Mistress Ellison. A proven witch.'

Ferris nodded. 'I had thought as much. It is not the common sport in England, even in such parlous times, to burn a woman alive for no reason.'

'There is a confession. You are not come from London to examine such . . .?'

'No. I am no clerk, Master Hewer. You were certain that the writ was well-drawn? She was guilty?'

'Yes. Oh, yes, indeed. There was no shadow of doubt in it.'

'A signed admission of her guilt.'

Hewer nodded, his adam's apple bobbing like a trapped coney in a tunnel. 'She put her mark to it. And she has named others. But the Witchfinder lacked the time to pursue the charges. I shall put them to the question myself. I have learned the ways.'

'Learned them from the Witchfinder? From the fine Master Monk?'

'From Master Monk, himself. He and . . . How knew you his name? Someone in the alehouse?'

'No.'

'Then . . . Ah, I think that you are Master Ferris. Captain John Ferris, of Hertford.'

'Let us go around the side of this barn, Magistrate Hewer, and you and I can talk more open, away from the eyes of the common rabble.'

The rain had eased once more. Hewer was about to protest until John let his right hand slip to the hilt of the sword, drawing it a scant inch from the sheath. Showing the bare metal, and then sliding it home again.

'We . . . Yes, indeed. But if you are the sworn enemy of Master Monk, as he told me, then you have no quarrel with me.'

'My quarrel is with Monk. He most villainously butchered both my dear father and my gentle mother. Having them falsely 'cused as witches.' He found it hard to speak of the matter, even so many months after. Unable to wipe the vision of the gibbeted corpses of his parents from his mind's eye.

'They were not . . .'

Ferris had pushed Hewer in front of him, around the corner of the tithe barn, out of sight of anyone. Now he swung him about, hard against the wooden wall.

And now he drew the blade all the way, holding it up so that the cold steel rested against the side of the land-owner's cheek, the tip close to his left eye.

'They were both saintly, good folks, Master Hewer. That dog Monk was not fit to lace their shoes. He roused the stupid and the vicious against them. Stole their life savings. And he also stole my betrothed Mary, forcing her to go with him on some threat or blackmail.'

'The slattern with the pipe was . . .'

'Liza Hall. And the brace of gippoes were the Mendoza brothers. I slew one of that foul brood some weeks back, before the arrant curs fled to France.'

'Then this other girl . . .'

'Mistress Mary Villers.'

'Has she hair that is long and fair?'

'She is still with them? I had thought that she might have picked some hope of 'scaping from their vile company. Yet, that she has not is sure token, Magistrate, of the hold he has on her.'

Hewer managed a weak smile, as if the words of John Ferris had prompted a jest.

'Surely it be a hold, and . . .'

'Guard that tongue, man, else I shall slit it and feed it to the dogs. Or roast it in that poor woman's pyre and feed it to you. Where has Monk gone?'

'Would you not know of the wench?'

'I know of her. And I will hear nothing from your tongue, thank 'e. Monk?'

'North.'

'London?'

Hewer started to shake his head, stopping when he discovered the action brought his face into sharp contact with the sword's keen edge. A tiny worm of blood appeared and crept over his cadaverous chin.

'No. But, Master Ferris . . . The girl that you spoke of as being abducted by . . .'

'I have warned you. Men such as you prey upon the weak and helpless, do you not? Lop the ears off sturdy vagabonds who rest a while in this place. Cold Easter, is it called? A cold welcome, do they have of it, Magistrate Hewer.'

'But I only . . .' The words were stopped short as Ferris brought the sword up and round and down in a lightning-fast movement. Cropping the skinny man's left ear clear away from the side of his head. Stepping back as the ear fell to the muddied earth and blood jetted against the lath and plaster wall of the barn.

Hewer opened his mouth to cry out and Ferris stepped in closer to him, bring his knee up into his groin, doubling the magistrate over like a fawning courtier. Breath rasped out and Hewer fell to his face, fighting for air.

'Now, Master Alexander Hewer, Squire of Kent. Butcher of witches. Burner of elderly dames. Tell me where friend Monk has taken himself and his mongrel crew. Right quickly or I shall spit you like the brutish hog that you are.'

'He said north.'

'Whither?'

'Across the Thames. Into Hertford and Essex, was what he said. Oh, my stomach. I swear my belly is quite torn apart. And my ear . . .'

'Lackaday, Sir,' mocked Ferris, poking the tip of the sword into Hewer's back, pinking him and making him wriggle in the dirt.

'I have told you what I know. Hertford and Essex. He told me of his many triumphs there.'

'Aye, that is sooth. Many a triumph. Might and lies and fear and threats and beatings, against the old and the frail and the lackbrains. Fine triumphs, Master Hewer.'

'I did not . . .'

'Not what?'

Hewer raised himself to hands and knees, blood streaming down the side of his narrow face. 'Spare me, Master Ferris. Go your way and I will hold my tongue on what you have done to me. I swear it.'

'You will tell no man of seeing me?'

Hewer shook his head, struggling for an expression of honesty.

Failing.

'Liar,' whispered the ex-soldier, thrusting the sword through the man's heart, the steel sliding effortlessly between his ribs, killing him instantly. Giving him the speedy mercy denied to Mistress Charlotte Ellison, whose corpse still smouldered only a few paces off.

Ferris wiped his sword in the grass and turned back towards his tethered mare.

'North, then' he said.

CHAPTER THREE

The Civil War grew less fierce as autumn began to drag its russet cloak across the tired land. The rain that fell during September turned tracks to streams and streams to turbulent, uncrossable rivers that foamed and surged at muddy banks.

From Hewer, John had learned he was truly still on the right trail for his vengeance. The months that had crept by since the deaths of his parents had not abated his lust for revenge on Robert Monk. The money that the witchfinder had stolen from him was of less importance, though it would, in truth, have eased life for him.

And there was Mary.

Gentle, sweet Mary, as soft and tender as fresh cream on a summer's morn. Hair of gold and eyes blue as corn-flowers. She would be twenty now, having had her birthday since Monk had taken her away.

And John Ferris wanted her.

Wanted her back again.

His relationship with her had been many things. Often fiery, but always seeded with love. God, but he loved her. Despite her coldly religious family of Puritans. Mary was the youngest of ten children, of which seven still lived. Her father, Jabez, was the

Widford stone-mason. His face and heart as inflexible and unyielding as the local flint.

John had eventually managed to win acceptance from the family. Even from the four untrusting brothers. Sober, dull men, who rarely laughed and seemed to find little pleasure in the brightness of the sun or the sound of a running stream. The twins, Reformation and Diligence Villers. Praise God, the oldest. And Seek Wisdom And Deny Sin Villers, perhaps the most intransigently religious of the whole family. The mother, Martha, had died of a bloody flux only two years ago, despite the best efforts of John's father, Thomas Ferris, to save her.

But the rest of them were only dim shadows compared to the dazzling daughter. The prettiest girl in all of Hertfordshire. Aye, and Essex too. She and he had loved each other.

Yet there had been something about the girl that had given John cause for some worry. Anxiety about the way she had behaved when locked into sexual congress with him. Then all of her graces would desert her and she would scream and rut like a Seven Dials whore, nails raking at his back, teeth set in his shoulder.

It frightened him, the intensity of her passion. And then he had heard word of the ways of the witchfinders. How a woman's wanton behaviour whilst making the beast with two backs could be read as signs of her pact with the Devil. How such a woman might have sold her immortal soul to the demons of darkness for the right to indulge herself in the base pleasures.

So, he had chosen to quieten their relationship. They still met, and there was never a shred of doubt that they would be wed. But he had not bedded her for some time before his accident.

And before Monk came slinking in like a midnight spectre to ruin everything.

What preyed most on John's mind was what it could be that kept his beloved Mary with the monster. What fiendish hold did he have over her that restrained her from running away from the witchfinder? And if he managed to rescue her, would he do some harm, in his innocence and ignorance?

These were bridges that must needs be crossed.

The weather seemed to worsen as he made his slow and cautious way north. If Monk had warned Hewer about him, as he clearly had, then the witchfinder must still fear that he was being pursued. And that could mean that a trap might be laid against him. There was so much suspicion in England in 1645 that it would not be difficult to lure him into some careful strategem.

It was tempting to go straight through London, but John suspected that Monk might avoid the city. His trade was one that could only flourish in country regions, where the writ of true law no longer ran, and the local justices had the real power.

There were clues that he was on the right path. A travelling tinker was sitting beside a merry fire, three days out of Cold Easter. A skinned rabbit was cooking and a battered bowl held some carrots and sliced turnips in boiling water.

'Good day and will you come and take all of my food, your honour?'

'What?'

'Will you have all of my meat and food?'

Ferris grinned at the man's cunning. 'You think that by offering all, I shall feel shamed and take none?'

The tinker grinned back. 'Indeed, but that's very truth, Captain.'

'You know me for a soldier?'

'Aye. Such a big strapping fellow can only be a soldier. Or a rogue. And I took you for the first, Captain, did I not?'

'I was a soldier, friend. But now I am an ordinary man. No rogue.'

'Then join me, Captain. And right welcome. Since I support the country against that royal rogue.'

'I might be a King's man?'

The tinker shook his head at that. 'I know a man, sir. And you are not for the King. Come. The coney is near done, and the stew will soon be well cooked. I have some bread I begged at an inn last eventide. I lack but the ale.'

Ferris swung from Morgana's back, tying her quickly to a nearby elm. Looking up at the leaden sky, grateful that the rain had held off for a few hours. He sat by the tinker and ate heartily of the stew, wiping his wooden platter clean with the crusty bread. Leaning back against the bole of the elm, flicking away some gnats that gathered about the smoke from the fire.

'You are for London, Captain?'

'No. I am for Hertford town where my parents did live. I have friends . . .'

'I am for Blackheath, from the Midlands. There is a fair on the Heath in a week, and good pickings for such as me. Nimble with my hands, if you take my meaning, Captain?' Rubbing the side of his nose with a slender finger and winking.

'A fair?'

'Aye.'

'I had a friend . . . He was to go with a fair . . . I wonder if . . .'

'I can give him a message, Captain.'

'No.' He considered. Changing his mind. 'Aye, friend. I would thank 'e for that.'

'His name?'

'York. Brutus York.'

'God's wounds! By Saint James of Compostella!' The tinker slapped himself hard across the knees, sending a cloud of dust into the air. 'The black!'

'Yes.'

'By the Blessed Virgin Bubonia of Ishmaelia! You, a friend of the black.'

'You have met him?'

'Aye, Captain.' Peering at Ferris from beneath lowered lids. 'I'll warrant you be a fine hand with a sword, Captain. Well-set and strong with it. But I would not wish to entwine with yon Brutus York. I swear he is the most powerful man I ever saw. Black or pink. Christian or Jew. God's wounds, Captain!'

'You have seen him this summer?'

'Aye. Right thankful, I was. A keeper of some noble lord's game came around the fair, brayin' out some tale or other of a salmon gone and some venison that had . . . The usual old tale, Master.'

'And Brutus?'

'The black came as the keeper was set to flog me. Usin' a great cudgel set with nails that would have left half my face upon it. Brutus picked up this girt keeper as easy as a new-born babby. Bent him over his knee, he did. Broke his back and dropped him in the dirt like a suit of clothin' he'd no use for.'

'Brutus killed the man?'

'And saved my skin, Captain. A good man, is the black. And I'm rightly glad that I was able to share my humble meal with his comrade. What is the message? I know he is to be at the fair.'

'Tell him that you have met with Captain John Ferris from Hertford town.'

'Captain John Ferris from the town of Hertford,' repeated the tinker. Thoughtfully picking at his teeth with a splinter of wood.

'And that I am on the trail of . . .' he hesitated at naming Monk. 'On the trail of my enemy. And will be in the land 'twixt Essex and Hertford in one week's time.'

'I'll do that, Captain. This enemy . . .? Would he be a man I know?'

Ferris bit his lip. Unsure of the tinker. Then deciding that he must take the chance on him.

'This must go no further than this place.'

'You have my word on it. And my word is as fine as any man, though my breeches be filled with holes.'

'His name is Monk, and he calls himself 'Witch-finder'. With him . . .'

The tinker held up a warning hand. 'E'en the trees have ears, Captain. I know Monk. He has two men with him. Romanies. Mendozas. Once there were three.' He brought his fist to his forehead in a sign against the evil eye. 'One was slain and the earth a better place for it.'

'I slew him, friend,' said Ferris.

'Then you have my hand and my heart,' replied the man, reaching out and clasping John's fist in both of his. 'They travel with a slut and another woman.'

'The other woman is my betrothed.'

'But . . .' It seemed as if the tinker was about to say more, but he checked himself and shook his head.

'What?'

'Naught of substance. I saw them two days back. There had been talk of a trial. But Master Monk was in a precious hurry to move on.' He laughed. 'The man is always seeking over his shoulder, as if he fears that the demons of Hell are at his back. Methinks it is your shadow, Captain, that he sees in every mirror and pool.'

Ferris sighed. 'Aye. The chase has been long and stern. Yet I am now closer than ever. But I fear he lays a trail of dragon's teeth behind him to try and snare me. I can trust nobody.'

'There is talk of a reward.'

'They say. Did he speak of where he was bound? I heard he intended for Hertford and the lands near Essex.'

The tinker seemed sunk in a reverie. 'What, Captain? I do beg your pardon, I had drifted off into a sea of my own foolish thoughts.'

'I asked if you knew where Monk was bound?'

'I think northwards. He talked of staying on Sunday night at the Pied Merlin at Barnswick.'

'Today is Thursday. I could be there by the evening of the Sabbath.' Ferris felt his heart begin to pound with excitement at the thought of being so close to his enemy.

And so close to Mary.

'They said there was a hundred guineas offered by Monk for your person, Captain,' said the tinker. 'It will tempt many a heart.'

'Not yours, friend?' smiled John.

Receiving a bright smile in return. 'Indeed, you may count upon that. As sure as my name is Orlando Logbane.'

Ferris rose to his feet. 'You say he will be there by Sunday? He is on the road until then?'

'Aye, Captain. Barnswick by Sunday. It would be wise to go by a track about the houses and hills. Avoid him. He has a cart and will be slow. You can be faster on that red-eyed mare.'

It was sound council. 'I shall. Now I must be on my way, Master Logbane.'

'The pleasure in this meeting has been mine, Captain Ferris. I shall give your message to the black, should I meet him.'

'Do so. I thank you for the stew.'

'God go with you, Captain,' called the tinker standing and kicking dirt over the ashes of his dying fire. Watching the ex-soldier as he mounted Morgana. Waving a hand as the sturdy figure disappeared along the woodland path, heading northwards.

A thousand feet in the cool autumn sky a peregrine falcon hung, motionless, riding the light winds. Staring down at the shimmering land far beneath. Seeing the man on the horse pushing on at an easy canter, circling around to the east to avoid a direct route to Barnswick. And by the smoking embers it saw the other man. Hastily harnessing a donkey to a little cart and whipping it away to the north.

Hurrying as if his life depended upon speed.

As if someone's life depended on his speed.

It was all a matter of no interest to the falcon.

CHAPTER FOUR

He heard the bells of the church, ringing out through the cool September evening when he was still better than three miles from Barnswick. The clear notes bringing back memories of happier times. Sunday services with his mother, caped and serene. His father, nodding to the locals as they tugged their forelocks to him, waiting by the wicket gate to their own flint-walled church.

It all seemed an eternity ago to John Ferris.

He set his heels to Morgana and the mare responded with a snicker of discontent. Shaking its head and slowing its gait.

'Get on. Mary and Joseph! You wilful harlot animal! Move on.'

Holding the reins in his left hand he leaned forwards along the neck of the mare, reaching out with his gauntleted right hand. Grabbing the silky soft ear nearest to him and giving it a savage tweak. Making Morgana whinny in protest and jump forwards as if he'd placed a thistle beneath its docked tail.

'Better, my dove. Better.'

It was close to dark, long shadows lurking at the bottom of the shedding bushes and hedges. Dry leaves rustled in the ditches, and in the cartwheel furrows on the track.

He had taken the advice of the tinker, using a circuitous route to reach Barnswick. Not wanting to get there too soon and lay himself open to the network of spies and informers that he now knew Monk was readying to entrap him.

A hundred guineas would be a wide field of loyalty from most men.

And it was small beer compared to the two thousand guineas that Monk had stolen from the Ferris home in Hertford.

The bells stopped and silence eased back over the land. Service would be starting soon, meaning that most of the inhabitants would be safe in church. And he could enter Barnswick snug from prying eyes. After his previous experiences he realised that his best course of action would be to find some barn or shed without the village, tethering the mare out of sight. A man on foot was less noticeable.

By the time he found what he sought, it was full dark, a hunter's moon floating large and silver over the fields of Barnswick. Showing him a derelict hay-barn, its roof mainly collapsed, but with one end still snug and dry. Morgana tried to bite him as he took off the bridle and John dealt it a ferocious buffet with his fist that made it stagger and nearly fall. He grinned at the mare, patting her on the smooth muzzle.

'You try, my beauty. But I still have the speed and the strength for you.'

He fetched water in a dented bucket he found in one corner of the barn, pulling a few handfuls of sweet grass for the horse. Slapping her on the flank and leaving her, heading for the centre of the village.

* * *

The Pied Merlin was easily found.

Barnswick was a fairly large community, surrounded by spreading, open fields, divided into countless narrow strips, some lying fallow, some cultivated. There was a narrow river winding through the centre, crossed by a low stone bridge. Perhaps five dozen cottages scattered higgledy-piggledy along the road, ending in the square-towered church.

And the alehouse.

A new building, the thatch still bright and fresh, paint on the wattle and daub standing out stark white in the moon-light. It was well-lit, golden blooms of warmth spilling into the lane outside the mullioned windows.

Only a couple of the cottages showed any sign of life, but John could hear the sound of singing coming lustily from the church. It had stained glass in the end wall and he stopped for a moment, his eyes caught by the beauty of the deep reds and blues.

On a sudden impulse John turned on his heel, walking back out of Barnswick. The night made him feel more vulnerable. If Monk were there, then he might have set a gin for him. And he was not about to place his neck in the witchfinder's noose.

He slept well that night, close by Morgana, waking early at first light.

'Come for 'trial, Master?' asked an elderly man in a stained smock, leaning against a crooked stile just outside Barnswick.

'The trial? Master Monk's work?'

The dotard grinned, showing a mouth filled with

more gaps than teeth. 'Aye, the blessed saint hisself. Sortin' out evil from good. Standin' as a shield to us poor folk agin them as worships evil.'

'Has he taken many witches?'

'Three. All kin. Live out beyond Vinegar Hill, top o' Mardock's Acre. Middletons. Wealthy. Thinks they's better than us. Word is of gold hid in their woods. Us'll find it, with help of Master Monk. They was took two days back. He and his merry men'll try 'em this noon-time. They's been walkin' 'em.'

Ferris knew about the way they walked witches. Keeping them on the move, for long hours on end. Often naked. Whipping and beating them if they tried to stop. Ignoring the wretches' bleeding feet. Not even allowing them pause for the calls of nature. It would have broken the spirit of many a hale and healthy fellow. But most of those accused of wizardry were close to their dotage, often in poor health. Which often resulted in speedy confessions and even speedier executions.

'They try them where?'

'Noon, Master. Did I not say that?'

'That you did. But where?' Raising his voice as the old man cupped his hand to his ear with an expression of almost manic concentration.

'If it be my age you ask, I be eighty summers and eight come next Candlemas.'

'No! No.' As the man recoiled from his vehemence. 'I did but ask you where these rogues were to be tested? At the inn?'

'The Pied Merlin, Master. That be it. But if ye is tardy, then there will be scant space. The trial will bring folks many a long mile.'

Ferris nodded. 'Aye, that I believe. The common herd will have their sport.'

'What?'

'Juvenal said that: "Duas tantum res anxius optat, panem et circenses". Rightly.'

'I cannot hear, Master. But I be eighty and eight years of age, come . . .'

'Bread and the circus, you old fool! That is all.'

He passed on, leaving the dotard scratching at his grizzled pate. Still muttering . . . 'Come next Candlemas, Master.'

The creaking sign outside the Pied Merlin showed an ill-painted bird of dubious parentage. Resembling a drowning chicken more than a colourful bird of prey. John realised as he walked up the street that he needed not have asked where the witch trial was taking place. The village of Barnswick was almost deserted, cottage doors standing open, despite the chill in the air. As he crossed the bridge, John paused and looked down over the low parapet.

The water was foaming as it rushed over a stone weir, cold and brown. Immediately beneath the bridge there was a deep and sheltered pool, fringed with long tendrils of green weed. Ferris shuddered at the grim look of the water, imagining sinuous pike or blind eels dwelling there among the clammy boulders.

He could hear the noise of the trial from a hundred paces off. A constant murmur of talk, broken by an occasional laugh. Once he heard what might have been a woman crying, but it was immediately drowned in bellowing merriment and he could not be certain.

As he walked up the main street of the village he could see that the alehouse was packed to its rafters. The windows at the front were open and men and women were leaning in. Children scampered in and out of the doorway, pushing their way between the legs of the watchers and listeners.

Ferris stepped to one side to avoid a pile of fresh horse manure. Steadying his sword as it trailed in the scabbard with a touch of the left hand on the hilt. As the weather grew worse, colder and more wet, John was more aware of the injury to his elbow. His father had warned him that it might stiffen and become sore during changes in the weather. It seemed that he was correct.

Tables had been set up outside the inn and people sat there, some eating, cramming hunks of bread into their mouths, washing it down with bumpers of foaming ale. As he grew nearer he saw one red-faced lout banging on the table and bellowing in a drunken voice. 'Burn 'em! Burn 'em all. Burn, burn, burn!!!'

A chant that was speedily taken up by every soul about the place until the tavern seemed to shake with the din.

'Bread and a circus,' said Ferris to himself, shaking his head at the vicious spectacle.

There was no possibility of gaining access to the Pied Merlin, even though the clock on the tower of the church showed barely ten minutes after the hour of noon. Hardly a head turned in his direction, everyone fascinated by what was taking place within the building.

John paid little attention to the other houses in Barnswick, concentrating on the inn.

So, he did not see a curtain twitching at the dormer window of a cottage directly across the street from the Pied Merlin. Nor see the pale face of a man behind the curtain. A tall man, with curling hair and a hooked nose. Standing among the crowd outside the inn Ferris didn't notice a figure cross the road behind him, slipping into a cribb'd alley that ran to the rear of the Pied Merlin.

Even had he seen him, John would have had little to fear. Robert Monk had seen him, but never clear. Nor had his minions seen him well enough to be certain of him again. Mary knew him, but she would never betray him.

Though the gipsy fellow had gone from the dormer window, there was still someone in the room. But the reflections of the leaded glass would have made it impossible to make out who it was.

But John Ferris knew nothing of this. All his attentions being directed through the windows of the inn, where his great height gave him the advantage of seeing over the heads of most of the crowd.

The prisoners were easy enough to spot. Three elderly people, sitting together at a narrow table, their hands roped behind them, halters about their necks. All of them, two men and a woman, showing signs around the face of having suffered severe beating.

'Monk,' whispered John, finally seeing the witchfinder.

Robert Monk was dressed in his habitual suit of quiet grey, even down to the elegant gloves. His hat lay on the table in front of him and he was talking in a quiet voice. Ferris could make out the local gentry, ranged on a high-backed settle flanking the fireplace, where some logs were burning with sullen resignation. There were three magistrates, listening intently to the evidence, all three showing their pride at being so central in such an important matter, near to so famous a man as Robert Monk, the Witchfinder himself.

John waited patiently among the crowd, eyeing his enemy. Wondering where he was staying, and what sort of an opportunity he might seize to kill the man. As he watched and listened he saw one of the Mendoza brothers come pushing into the tavern from some rear entrance, stooping low at the side of Monk. Putting his hand to his mouth and whispering in his ear. The Witchfinder nodded, his eyes flicking up for a moment from the parchment in front of him, then nodding once more. It seemed to John as if his eyes locked with those of Monk, but it could only have been his imagination.

Nearly a half hour passed by. It was hard for those outside in the street to hear some of the evidence, particularly when the accused trio were answering questions. But the replies were passed back by those better able to hear.

It was the usual clap-trap that John had heard before. Tales of bewitchment of husbands by the old woman. Of women by the men, and of urging in the night to strange, unnatural acts. Of giant members, feeling as if they were of leather filled with burning ice, that thrust into the privy parts of the innocent of Barnswick.

Familiar spirits that spread mischief and malice all about. Brindled cats that mewed in the night and brought chancres to sleeping babes.

Ferris stood and listened, wishing that he had

thought to bring food with him to succour him through what was obviously destined to be a long and wearisome day. With Monk tethered to the trial, it was a monstrous temptation to go out and seek Mary. But he could see only Liza Hall. Sitting behind the prisoners; leading the mocking laughter. Neither of the Mendozas was there.

Having nearly been caught once before, Ferris wasn't about to make a fool of himself by rushing winking to his own doom. Patience was a safer game.

Monk asked for a break for an hour, saying he wished to discourse further with the witches, and the inn was cleared. John immediately moved away, contenting himself with walking back to the barn, and taking out some dried meat for sustenance.

Returning in time to secure a place for himself within the Pied Merlin, on a bench that was placed just in front of a window. Once again Liza Hall took her position behind the accused, and Monk sat at his own table close by the gentry. The Mendozas were once again absent.

Monk rose to his feet, looking unusually pleased with himself. John wondered whether he had managed to persuade the three Middletons to confess and save himself time and money. Or they had perhaps told him of the hiding-place of the legendary crock of gold and offered it him in exchange for their freedom.

Nothing surprised him about the man called Monk.

'My lords, good people of Barnswick. During this last hour, for which I crave all of your indulgences,' bowing to the three magistrates. 'During this time I have been locked in deep converse with these three miserable wretches. They know that they face a fearful end of being put to the stake and burned while still living. Not to mention other ways in which I might question them further. But if they were to aid me in my queries, then I have sworn that they shall be spared all this.'

There was immediate hubbub. An elderly woman at John's side leaped to her feet, protesting that they should all be burned. 'And drawn and quartered first, Master Monk. Thou shalt not suffer . . .'

Monk held up his hand for quiet. 'I know, good dame. I shall not suffer a witch to live. But, I can aid their passing. A speedy end with the hemp collar. Or the slow fire?'

'Burnin', for 'em!' was the immediate response. John looked around, seeing the feral gleam of sheer hatred in the eyes of the peasants jostling around him. The crowd beyond the window also called out their anger for the trio of witches. Turning to stare behind him, Ferris thought for a moment that he caught a glimpse of one of the Mendoza brothers, lurking among the mob, but the people moved and shifted and the gypsy disappeared. If he had ever been there.

'My friends,' shouted Monk, holding up a gloved hand once more. 'Friends of Barnswick. There is yet more to be told. These wretches are not the leaders of their coven. They have a stranger who is their lord and master and who speaks to Satan for them.'

'What stranger?' called a voice from behind John, out in the street.

'Aye, name him!' bellowed someone else.

'I shall. For they have sworn to me that he is here in

Barnswick now. They have seen him. He came to them in their cells last night, despite all guards. Whispered to them that he would free them with maleficent spells and enchantments. So, I have promised them that they shall hang before this day is done and their suffering shall be brief.'

There was a momentary silence in the village and John could catch the distant chuckling of the water beneath the bridge.

'Name him!'

'They say his name is John Ferris and he sits by the window of this inn.'

John clearly heard the double click as a pair of pistols were cocked close by him, and he felt the coldness of steel against the back of his neck.

CHAPTER FIVE

'He is not to be harmed.'

For such a mild-seeming man, Robert Monk possessed a voice of chilling ferocity. He rarely raised it, yet both the gipsies pulled away from their helpless captive as though hot irons had been applied to their spines.

'Not a mark. There will be time enough, lads, for such sport.'

'But we . . .'

'I know, Daniel. I know. Our young and impulsive prisoner has done much that seeks a settlement. There will be time enough. That I swear to you.'

'The scores lies 'twixt thee and me, Monk,' spat John. 'None other.'

'You slew our brother, Benjamin,' replied Daniel Mendoza, face working with his anger. A great vein stood out, throbbing, across his forehead, and his fingers were clenched into fists.

'He attacked me.'

'It is a matter of small interest,' sighed Monk. 'For within two weeks this will be all in the past. Master Ferris, or what little remains of him from the ashes, will be finished and we shall all be free of his shadow that has set at our backs overlong.'

'Two weeks.'

'Aye, Liza. A sennight to the town of Hertford. It is meet that the pup shall die where his parents did. And a bare sennight to his ending.'

The woman laughed. Tweaking Ferris on the cheek. 'I shall keep close guard on him. May I sport with him, Monk?'

'He is not be marked or harmed, you damned harlot, Liza! You may do as you will, but I fear me that your games are too rough for him. I want a full man for trial. Not a mewing creature that you have unmanned.'

'I will . . .'

'No. I think that you shall go first with me to the north. Daniel, you shall guard him with Abe. But your life is forfeit if he is hurt. I swear that you will both die if he is marred.'

'You shed no tears, Robert, for the others we catch at their evil.'

The witchfinder nodded. 'Truly, Abraham. But this is not a whining baggage that nobody cares for and who is without position and learning. Captain Ferris is an officer and, save the mark, close to a gentleman. I go ahead and I will prepare our case against the master wizard.'

John Ferris was clothed, which was a blessing to his pride. But iron collars secured his wrists and ankles together, a sturdy chain linking the cuffs to a great ring-bolt set in the wall of the barn where he was kept.

'You mean that you go to bribe and set your poisons to snare the fools and the greedy and the gullible so that they will lie about me.'

'You were caught as easy as a frost-bit robin falling from a branch.' Monk came a step closer to him. 'You have been a wen upon my life too long, Master.'

'And you to mine. My parents butchered. My rightful gold stolen. And my betrothed spirited away by you.'

'Mary Villers!' Monk seemed genuinely surprised at the accusation.

'You cannot say she is not with you!'

'No.'

'Then?'

'Then she is with me. Mayhap you will see her. I send her ahead of us so, in Hertford?'

'And there you still keep your throttling links about her fair neck, you damnable cur. Lickspawn filth. Hedge-drinker! Gutter-foulness!'

'I must be gone.'

'The magistrates . . .' interrupted Liza Hall, tapping out her clay pipe on the heel of her shoe.

'Ah, truly. It was a neat subterfuge, was it not, John Ferris? Well laid and well-sprung. Word came to me from a travelling man that were bound this way.'

'The tinker! Mary and Joseph but he seemed a friend to me!'

'He was not a Romany, Ferris,' sneered Abraham Mendoza.

Daniel grinned, showing a fine set of strong white teeth. 'Aye, and he said to tell you that he grieved mightily for givin' you up to us.'

'But a man must live,' chimed in Liza Hall.

'And he did say that if it might tip the balance a little his way in your favours, he would see your message was passed on within three days.'

That news was scant help to John, now securely imprisoned. Knowing how dangerous he might be, the gipsies would give him little hope of escape. Yet . . . if the tinker truly sought out Brutus York, and the black was prepared to come and . . . But that was a maid's thoughts. A man might as well piss into the gale.

'The magistrates, Robert,' repeated the woman, delving busily among her enormous, sagging breasts, catching some tiny creature, and cracking it between her finger and thumb.

'Yes. Those three fools will hang before the church service this evening. That is their reward for playing the part well that I had coached them for. I had spies out for you, from a house across from that stinking inn.'

It bothered Ferris to wonder who might know him well enough to betray him to the witchfinder. Not the Mendozas and not the slut. Perhaps the tinker had described him with sufficient detail for the spies Monk spoke of. But it still seemed . . .

'Barnswick would feel greatly cheated if a witch taken in their own alehouse was not to be tested here before being stolen away to Hertford town.'

'What?'

Monk shook his head and repeated what he had just said. 'I fear me you should pay less scant attention, John Ferris. They wish to see you swum.'

'You said at Hertford!'

Ferris was a brave man, but the calm, expressionless face of Monk as he spoke of 'swimming' was enough to turn his bowels to water.

'Aye. And so you shall be. That is where we shall all meet once more. Where you might see your

Mistress Villers that was so cruelly ravished against her wishes.'

'Aye, Robert,' laughed Liza Hall. 'Yet not so . . .'

'Hold your tongue, woman,' snapped Monk, shutting her off in mid-sentence. 'She will be there. So will this poxed bag of sweating tripes, so you are safe from her for a week or more. The Mendozas will not hurt you. And I ask you to tell me if they should be less than well-mannered to . . .'

'Master Monk!' exclaimed Daniel Mendoza.

'Well-mannered to you.'

'Then why must I be swum? You know that I am no witch.'

Despite his own horror John struggled to maintain self-control. Despite all his efforts he could recognise the note of pleading that had crept into his voice unbidden.

But even as he spoke he saw what a waste of time it was. Monk's face was set as inflexibly as cold granite and there would be no deflecting him from his purpose.

John sighed and squeezed his eyes shut. Finding himself suddenly on the brink of tears.

'We will swim you, wizard Ferris, before noon on the morrow. May you sleep well this night.'

There was to be little sleep.

The barn was cold. Rain came around midnight, pattering on the worn thatch, finding its way between the cracks, dripping on the straw and dirt beneath. Monk had ordered that John should be fed with a bowl of luke-warm stew, ladled for him by Liza Hall. Watched closely by Daniel Mendoza so that she couldn't indulge her pleasures. But as she wiped his mouth with a greasy cloth the middle-aged wanton whispered to him.

'I'll be back, later, lover. Back later my proud soldier.'

It was a threat, not a promise. After the meal the gipsy brothers tested his chains, taking care to keep their own bitterness on a tight rein. But as they worked they talked softly to each other in their own Romany tongue. Occasionally breaking out from it to remind him of the horrors of the trial that was to come within seven days. Promising him that even a confession would not spare him.

'Own up, Captain, and we'll both stand and swear on a stack of testaments that you was put up to it by your Satan and that truly you believe you are not guilty of the charges.'

'We don't want you slippin' away easy.'

'No, Abe, indeed we do not.'

'Hard is what we want.'

'Real hard. There's nasty things we know 'bout that us can do with needles.'

'Verily, Daniel, we can. Them small hooked ones that heat up red as a cherry and slip behind the ball of the eye.'

John Ferris stood against the rough wall of the barn and tried to ignore their cruel banter. Tried to shut away from his mind the certain knowledge that they spoke little but the truth. He had seen and heard enough during his pursuit of Monk and his crew to know that there was very little in the ways of inhumanity that they would not use.

'What of cutting at the sinews of his wrists and his knees, brother?'

'Sinews?'

'So that he can move no more than a lamed beggar. And blind him.'

'One eye or both?'

Daniel Mendoza considered the question. 'Both, be best, eh?'

'His tongue?'

'Slit and drawn.'

'Ears?'

'Lopped and cropped.'

'Aye. Peel some skin and push peppercorns beneath it. Make him run on them.'

Daniel laughed at the suggestion. 'And tie him over a table.'

'The dogs, you speak of?'

'Aye, good brother. Get the dogs to use him as they would a bitch.'

'Teach him.'

'A lesson,' nodded Daniel. 'Teach the bloody-handed murderer a fine lesson to draw on his slate.'

'Let me just cut him a little about . . .' began the taller of the two.

But his brother checked him with a warning whistle. 'If Robert Monk finds his goods are sullied, then it will be our heads next to roll. Our skin blistering in the flames. Our necks stretched by the rope.'

'Then we'll leave him to his silvery slumbers, brother.'

They went out, arms about each other, tugging the heavy door of the barn close shut behind them. Sliding a massive iron bolt across to keep it locked.

John had already made some attempts to shift the chains that held him, but he had finally ceased his efforts, recognising how vain they were, deciding that he would do better to save his strength for what opportunity the future might bring him.

Trying to keep his mind off the morrow and the cold, deep water.

Sinuous pike.

Blind eels.

He found it hard to even achieve a position that did not pain him. The chain around his neck cut under his jaw every time that he tried to turn his head or ease himself. And the irons about ankles and wrists were already chafing him.

He saw the light outside before he heard any sound of steps. A golden glow that appeared at the bottom of the door, streaming out across the floor of the barn. His first thought was that the Mendozas were going to ignore Monk's orders to them and simply slit his throat. Perhaps taking their revenge first. Much might be done with two sharp knives in the hours of darkness to a helpless prisoner.

His second, fleeting, thought was that Brutus York had come. The tinker had kept his word – part of his word – and taken the message to the black.

But immediately he realised how low his spirits must have sunk to follow such a foolish thought. Even if that glimmer had been a spectre of hope, there was utterly no way that the word could have gone that fast.

The door opened quietly and swung shut, giving him only the barest glimpse of a figure, holding a hooded lantern. It looked like a woman, cloaked.

'Mary?' he whispered.

The lantern was placed on the dry earth, the shutter slid nearly shut. So that there was precious little light in the barn. But his eyes were suited to the blackness and he could just see that the woman was coming closer to him.

'Mary? Is that you, my dearest?'

If it were, then they could both be free and away within the hour. John's heart leaped to his throat at the thought. After so much waiting it could be a miraculous ending. From despair to elation in the space of a handful of seconds.

'Mary, my sweet dove.'

There were fingers at the front of his breeches, fumbling at the lacing. Groping at him.

'Mary?'

'Shut your fuckin' gob, cully, or I'll slice your cock clean off!'

It was Liza Hall.

There was nothing that he could do to check her using him in any way she wanted. The only minimal sparing grace was that he was tethered standing, making it impossible for her to get him flat on his back where she really wanted him.

But she did what she could.

Freeing him from the confines of his breeches, gripping him between her hard fingers. Using her nails along the length of his penis, pressing her body against his. Whispering to him of the obscenities she wished to perform.

'Leave me alone.'

'You thought I was that simpering straw-headed dolly! Why wish for her? Water in her body, not real blood. She is full busy this night, Master Ferris. And every night.'

'What do you mean, slut?'

He struggled to free his hands, the chains rattling in the cool of the night. But the gipsies had done their work well and he could barely move at all.

'It's for me to know and for you to hazard, ain't it? I shall say no more, Captain.'

'Leave me. Monk warned . . .'

'Bull's pizzle to him, Captain! Monk is cunning enough to know that I shall take care and care enough. Them gyppoes are good for some things, and he scares the dung from 'em. Not me.'

She hung against him, locking both arms around his neck. Liza was a heavy woman and her weight was near enough to strangle him. The chain about his neck tightened and he gasped for breath, feeling the pressure on his lungs.

'There, cully. See what little Liza can do for you. Make you pant for me, eh? Them gyppoes don't have the sense of a pig's arse. Good for some things. I been swivin' with both of 'em this night, drunken sots. Dan could barely lift himself for me. And that Abe was little better. Poor dead Ben was best for that. A fine stallion he was with me, ridin' in me saddle for a long mile every night. And you did for him, you bastard!'

Suddenly grabbing him by the testicles, making his body tense in shock. Tightening her fingers so that he breathed hard and shallow. Liza giggled as she lifted him to his toes, pulling him up.

'One twist and no more Captain Ferris, dear

dove,' she sniggered. 'So easy. But first a touch of pleasure for me, cully. I been done but twice and that's not what I want. It barely cools my itchin'. She moved away from him and he could hear her; burrowing beneath her skirts. Then her hand touching his face, making him flinch as if she'd slapped him.

'Want a taste of their love-juice, Captain? Right sticky, it be, 'twixt my legs. If only you wasn't tied so well and . . . I could make you . . .'

Despite her size and age, Liza Hall had a desperate agility, wriggling herself up on on him, using her fingers to guide him into her waiting warmth. John Ferris was utterly revolted by her grossness, yet his body responded to her obscene blandishments, quite beyond his control.

He had never felt more ashamed than during those interminable hours as the slattern used every one of her malign skills to make him do what she wanted. Time spun around him and he could no longer recall what the hour might be.

One moment the woman was hanging about his shoulders, gross thighs spread to encompass him, digging her heels into him. Then she was kneeling, using fingers and lips with a sickening expertise, sucking him drier than summer dust.

At last it was over.

And the woman was standing in front of him, one nail tracing a pattern from the corner of his eye to the edge of his dry, sore lips.

'You did well, Captain Ferris. Very honourable and brave. I shall mention you in my despatches for your valour and upstanding courage.'

'I beg you to leave me.'

'Aye, I will.'

'And never mention what has passed between us to a living soul.'

In the dimness he could catch the flash of white from her teeth as she smiled at him. Pinching his cheek with a familiar gesture, as if she were a maiden aunt, with her favourite nephew.

'You keep them lips tight shut in front of Master Monk, and it'll be our little secret to plight together, Johnny.'

She picked up the lantern, opening the shutter a half inch, so that a narrow blade of gold came darting out, making him blink. Still chained upright, his breeches carefully relaced, he watched as the woman walked towards the barn doors, opening them. Showing that the first pale light of dawn was breaking over Barnswick.

'I trust you'll relish your swim, cully,' she whispered. 'I and the wench will see you once more in Hertford town. Fare thee well, Johnny Ferris.'

And the door shut and Liza was gone. The bolt rattling behind her as she locked the barn.

Leaving Ferris alone again, with his thoughts. His thoughts of the horror of what was to happen to him during the coming day in that blind-black pool beneath the bridge.

And his thoughts of what had happened during the night.

The worst of it, that he could never ever admit to anyone, was that he had found parts of it enjoyable. That was the ultimate horror.

CHAPTER SIX

'Methought . . .'

Naked, cold, swirling, circling. The laughter tearing at his ears from the watchers around.

'Methought what . . .'

Dragged out, half-carried by the Mendozas. Monk there, urging, ordering them. Followed by a priest, red-faced, blood on his chin where he'd cut himself shaving too hastily on a chill morning.

'Methought what pain . . .'

The rest of Barnswick following, dressed as if it was a holiday. A high day. Whooping and singing, the girls in their best gowns and prettiest shoes. Some with garlands of autumn leaves woven into their hair as they danced around the bound man, mocking his helplessness.

'Methought what pain it . . .'

As they stopped on the bridge, a carriage, closed and curtained, rattling past and halting. Driven by Liza Hall, smoking clay pipe jammed between her teeth. Grinning down at John Ferris and winking at him. He was fighting against being stripped, but he glimpsed a hand pulling an edge of a curtain back and a face peering out at him. But it was too deep in shadow for him to make out who it was, but it crossed his mind that it might be Mary.

'Methought what pain it was . . .'

'Bind him widdershins,' called Robert Monk, and Daniel Mendoza pulled a couple of lengths of thin, strong whipcord from his belt.

He was held firmly by the Mendozas, but Monk was taking no chances. Keeping him covered with his own miquelet pistol, hammer cocked and ready. John's right thumb was bound tightly to his left big toe. Left thumb to right toe, so that he was doubled over, head between his knees.

'In with 'im,' called someone.

'It must be done in a proper manner,' retorted Monk, calmly. As unflustered as if someone had suggested that they might all enjoy a glass of wine before church.

'Methought what pain it was to . . .'

'Lower him upon my word.'

The priest was reading something from a large volume, but Ferris wasn't able to catch the words. Not even certain if it was the Bible or not. Monk held up his gloved hand again and the priest fell silent.

'I would say, Reverend, to the folk of Barnswick that they will now see a true testing of a witch. If Captain John Ferris is truly a witch.'

'The Lord God in the infinity of His great wisdom will surely judge.'

Monk nodded at the priest's unctuous interruption. 'Verily. Judge both the quick and the dead. If the witch should be thrown into deep water and shall float, it is then proven to us all that he is surely a witch. For only a witch, calling on his unholy Lord can avoid sinking beneath the waters to witness the great mysteries that flourish there.'

'Amen,' added the priest, most piously.

'Then in with him,' shouted a young man with a fearful squint.

'But if he should sink, gentles all,' continued the witchfinder, 'then he is judged to be innocent and free from wickedness and guile.'

John Ferris was still crouched in the dirt, pulling at the cords the gypsy had tied. Finding them less tight than he had thought. There was some play between thumbs and toes. Not enough to break free, but enough to give a degree of movement. It was puzzling that they should have slipped up in that way. Behind him, Monk was reaching the close of his short speech, but Ferris paid precious little attention to the words. All of his energy was concentrated on those two lengths of thin, waxed cord.

'So, should he break the surface, and struggle in the air, he is a witch, and shall be taken by us to his town of Hertford for trial as the leader of a coven there. The town where his dame and sire were both hanged as witches and warlocks.'

'It is not . . .' began John.

'Over and in,' called Monk and Ferris was hefted in the air and dropped suddenly from the low parapet of the bridge.

The shock was worse than he had feared. Worse than all of his night's imaginings.

The force of his fall turned him over and he was blinded in the murky waters. Unable for a moment to decide what was up and what was down. He felt long weeds brush their icy tendrils across his cheek, the roughness of slimy stones against his naked groin. In panic terror he almost opened his mouth to scream, but he clung to vestiges of control. Cold water filled his nose and down into his mouth.

He fought with total desperation, despite the impossible handicap of the hobbling ropes. Managing to bring himself towards the bright autumn air. Seeing light, dappled and mirrored. Fought for it, his head coming out for a tantalising moment.

'He swims!!!' came the cry from a hundred throats. From the peasants who lined the banks of the muddy river.

'The witch swims!!!'

But he did not.

He could not straighten his legs to kick his way again to the surface, and he sank once more. Closing his eyes and pulling at the twine with all his strength. Feeling it yield a little.

Up once more to a hubbub of yells.

And down, toppling into darkness.

His lungs seemed to be bursting as he fought for more air. His head was pounding, a band of iron about his temples. And he knew that he could not survive for long in the icy deeps.

The cord gave a few inches more.

More.

Despite the horror of his situation, John Ferris had won control over his fear. And he saw now, with a bitter clarity, how cunning Monk had been. Had he drowned, then there would have been no fine trial at Hertford. And someone might even have plunged in to save him.

So the brothers had been told to deliberately leave the cords slack. Just loose enough for a man fighting for life to be able to pull clear so that he could swim to the air.

'He is out!!! The witch swims!!!!'

There was sufficient play now between his toes and thumbs for him to be able to kick and tread water. Drawing in great soughing gulps of the cold morning air. Oblivious to the shouts and few stones that were now being hurled at him.

Oblivious to Monk calling out that the witch was truly tested and would be haled to Hertford. All John knew was that he had survived the ordeal with his life.

As he rested against the slippery bank, his lips moved.

'Methought what pain it was to drown,' he said.

CHAPTER SEVEN

'Young Johnny pinned Betty hard down to the floor,
And with his great gimlet began for to bore,
Just then, in the midst of his fingerin' and thumbin',
'Lord help us!' cries she, "There's someone a'comin'." '

The song seemed interminable, with a limitless variety to its verses. In the five days since they had left Barnswick John Ferris had heard every one of them. Daniel Mendoza had heard it in a tavern in Cheapside when last in London and was so enamoured with the bawdy ditty that he kept singing it at every turn of the road. Even his brother, Abraham, was heartily sick of it and had ridden on ahead of the cart.

John was chained at wrist and ankle, secured by a collar of iron to a ringbolt set firmly in the floor of the rattling wagon. And there he stayed. Twice a day he was allowed to relieve himself into a leather bucket and twice a day the gipsies fed him. Oatmeal gruel and bread. With water.

Monk was going on during each day, meeting up with them at an agreed alehouse each night. The women had pressed straight for Hertford, and were probably close to the town by now. Daniel had told Ferris that they expected to get to the town in three more days.

'Then the sportin' begins, friend,' he'd hissed.

The weather was turned cold, with sheets of steel rain driving in from the east on the teeth of a blustery wind. It rattled on the canvas of the cart, making it sound like a schooner beating up to Wapping against a gale.

The only minimal compensation that John could find in his misery was that the brothers had been kept in their places by Monk's orders and neither of them had even laid a hand upon him. Both made much play of spitting in his food and they had threatened twice to urinate in his drinking water. Since it was mainly drawn from muddied ditches anyway, he would have been hard-pressed to notice if they had done it.

There were only two thoughts that brought the least prospect of hope to John Ferris.

One was that his dearest Mary might be able to find some way of rescuing him. While he was kept in the wagon there was little chance of that. Daniel Mendoza kept the keys to the locks and chains on a hook at the side of his seat, well out of John's reach. But when they came to Hertford there might be friends or relations that Mary could enlist on his behalf.

And, fainter than a candle a'top a distant hill, he clung to the thought that Brutus York might somehow hear of his plight and come to aid him.

'And Johnny kept poundin', with no show of
fear,

When Betty tugged at his hair and called in his ear.
"Lord help me, Johnny, I'm no fiddle for flickin' or strummin',
If you don't stop that soon, then someone is comin'." '

They were only a day's ride away from Hertford. Robert Monk had heeled on ahead of them once they were well north of the Thames, to prepare the local gentry for the coming trial. And to ready the evidence that would be presented against John Ferris.

'I am hungered,' called John.

'Eat your own dung, witch,' replied Daniel Mendoza, laying his whip to the back of the ambling nag that drew their cart.

'Will we reach the town this night?'

'No.'

'The morrow?'

'Aye. You are right eager to reach your own doom, you bloody bastard whorin' dog! We shall be there before the mid of the day. Then to the dungeons there. And we can at last begin to pay a little of the score owin' for the killing of Benjamin.'

'Where shall we rest this night?'

They were approaching an area that John knew well, and he wondered which village would see them.

'Tonight we camp out. Master Monk does not wish word of our arrival to reach the people until he is ready to slip the news. So we sleep among the es.'

It made little difference to John where they stayed. All he had to look forward to was the inside of the cart.

Daniel hissed between his teeth, starting yet again to sing a verse of the tavern ballad.

' "Oh, no," said Johnny, "That can't be, I'll tell
you for sure.
For I've slid back the bolts on this side of the
door."
But Betty had none of this, sayin': "You stop
all that hummin'.
I'll tell you one last time there's somebody
comin'." '

During the afternoon the weather brightened and the sun broke through the high clouds. It became warm beneath the canvas and John considered asking Mendoza to remove it and allow him some fresh air. But he guessed, rightly, that the gipsy would ignore him.

The tail was unlaced and he could see out, watching the track wind away behind them, the horse's hooves clopping up curling skeins of dust. There was little traffic on the road, though he once saw a rider moving fast, leading a spare horse. Approaching within a couple of hundred paces, then halting. Turning off among the trees and disappearing from his sight.

He could see Mendoza and he noticed that the big man had also seen the rider. Reaching down and loosing the pistol from his belt. John Ferris's own miquelet lock gun, made by Ripoll of Catalonia. But he relaxed as the galloper vanished.

They stopped only minutes before evening slithered into night. The sky was clear with the promise of a frost later, and Mendoza loosed John's neck from the ring-bolt, dragging him from the bed of the wagon, tying him with a hemp rope to one of the wheels.

'This is the last night that ever you'll spend beneath the stars, Captain,' said the gypsy, tugging hard on the knots to make sure he was well tied. 'It is my kindness to you that I allow you to spend it thus.'

'I thank you.'

'And may you freeze to death, you bastard!' grinned Mendoza, raising a great ham of a fist, then holding back the blow. 'Nay, they shall see you unsullied when we ride into Hertford. As Robert Monk commanded. Then me and Abe will have our days and nights with you.'

Abraham Mendoza joined them. Eating a snatched meal of eggs, beaten with some cream and herbs. Cooked over a fire that his brother had built. Ignoring the helpless prisoner. But John overheard the conversation, learning that Monk was anxious that nothing should go amiss on the morrow. And he had ordered Abe to go on that very night and work with him, preparing for the entry into Hertford town.

Within a half hour he was mounted again, ready for off. Looking around the clearing where the cart was standing, the horse tethered to a nearby leaning pine.

'Take care, brother.'

'I will, Abe.'

'And watch for ghouls in the night.'

'Ghouls?'

'Demons, little Daniel. Night-crawlers that suck the blood from mortal men.'

'Sod off away, you sheep-fuckin' bugger! Go 'ere I give you a buffet that loosens your scant brains yet further.'

He ripped up a great clod of turf and heaved it at his brother, who laughed and rode off at a fast canter, vanishing from the circle of firelight. They could hear the sound of the hooves as they faded along the trail to the north.

John Ferris had noticed several occasions since his capture that had showed the deeps of superstition that languished in the soul of the gypsies. Both of them were frequently making small signs with hands or fingers to try and avert bad luck, both of them positively jingling with a variety of charms and amulets.

Though Daniel Mendoza made every effort to keep up his spirits, singing quietly and whistling to himself, Ferris saw that the jesting shaft about the place being the haunt of demons had struck the gold. The tall, curly-haired gipsy was obviously disturbed, and he threw more kindling on the fire to try and build up a larger circle of light. The flames danced and crackled, but they simply deepened the pools of shadows that dwelled between the trees all about them.

Despite the cold that began to bite into him well before midnight, John was still pleased to be out in the open. In his heart he recognised that he was doomed. Only in the ballads and tales told around the fire by old men did rescue come at the blowing of a horn, or at the sending of a magic arrow across an enchanted ocean. By the afternoon of the morrow he would be secured in durance vile, locked away behind stout walls, with rescue faded to a wisp of smoke that danced in the wind.

Daniel had broached a second flagon of ale that he had brought with him from the previous tavern. He lay back by the fire, singing quietly to himself, but every sound from the woods all about brought him up sharp. Sitting and reaching for the pistol that rested near the fire.

Ferris watched him, amused by the fear. Every now and again he cautiously pulled his head to one side, wondering whether the rope might be loosened. But this time he had been tied properly, with no intention of being allowed to break free. The knot didn't budge by a fraction of an inch.

Mendoza started to sing the bawdy song about Johnny and Betty, lingering over each verse. His words slurring as the liquor took its toll. He pounded his fist on the ground at the last line of every stanza, his voice becoming louder and louder.

Louder.

Reaching the penultimate verse, drawing breath ready for the climax.

The mug falling from his nerveless fingers. Jaw sagging and a strangled gasp of fear filling the stillness.

Both he and John Ferris could hear the voice. Beginning quietly, then gathering force over that last verse. Seeming as if it came from everywhere. From everywhere and from nowhere.

'Just then Johnny bored her so well, she began to
spend,
And Betty moaned and rolled so hard, it seemed
it would not end.
She spread wide her legs and her waters flowed
free,
Sayin': "Told you, Johnny. Someone's come . . .
and it's me!" '

The voice had an odd quality to it. It seemed to tumble and echo about itself, as it was being propelled through a long, twisting tunnel of iron. It had a startling effect on Mendoza.

He leaped to his feet like a rabbit put up by a reaper's sickel. Hefting the pistol and firing off a blind shot into the black woods about him. The gun cracked, the explosion flat in the open, and a puff of smoke came billowing from the muzzle. White, tinged with scarlet in the light of the moon and the fire. The ball whined off, richochetting from the trunk of one of the trees, then burying itself in the earth with a wet, thunking sound.

'Who . . .?' shouted Mendoza.

The voice floated from the other side of the clearing. Nearer than before.

'Someone's comin', Johnny, and it's me!'

'Who's there? That you, Abe? Is it, you damned rascal? Better that you . . .'

'Someone's comin', Mendoza, and it's *me*!'

The gipsy drew a thin-bladed knife and began to back off, towards the fire, eyes searching around for the taunting voice. Ferris felt that there was something vaguely familiar about the singer, but he could not lay his tongue to a name.

'I'll slit your fuckin' tripes from your guts, whoever you are. Show yourself. Be you man or monster!'

'And it's *me*!!!!'

The unseen stranger raised his voice to an eldritch shriek, the sound tearing at the cold night.

And he appeared.

John had once seen a fly trapped in a piece of amber. Frozen for ever in the yellow stone, a shard of time caught in the ice of infinity.

At that second, time seemed to stop, in the frosty clearing. Even the flames that danced in the fire slowed their movement. Daniel Mendoza dropped his knife, falling to his knees with a sigh of horror, hands going to cover his eyes.

It was nightmare incarnate.

A living terror to strike at the bowels of any human being.

The creature was tall. Heavily muscled. Naked. The eyes were circled in white, and streaks of crimson came from jagged teeth. The ends of the fingers were white bone, red-tipped. The bones of the thighs and chest were also outlined in vivid white. There were feathers stuck in the curly hair and a great spear flourished in the right hand. As it leaped into view it gave a terrifying banshee wail, hopping towards Mendoza, uttering a fearsome, guttural chanting.

And it was black.

Beneath the paint the gleaming skin of the monster was black as jet, smooth as ebony.

Black.

The name trembled on John Ferris's lips, but he

resisted calling out. Knowing that to do that might be to break the spell. Might release Mendoza from his terror.

'It's me.'

This time, said quietly. A sibilant whisper. Hardly rustling the air with its passing.

The apparition advanced a couple more paces, the spear hefted, ready to throw. Ready to strike the cowering gypsy clean through the centre of his breastbone.

'Nooooooooooooo . . .'

The anguished cry climbed and fell, tearing at the ears like a fingernail drawn down a broken slate.

Daniel Mendoza rose from his knees, leaving the knife and pistol where they'd fallen. Averting his gaze from the ghastly figure beyond the fire. Stumbling away from it, towards the horse and the protection of the trees.

The giant black drew the spear back, ready to hurl it at the fleeing man, then checked the throw as Mendoza stumbled and nearly fell.

'Go, dog, and never return to this sacred place!' bellowed the voice.

John saw that it held a strangely twisted piece of glittering metal to its lips, to create the distorted echo that had sounded so terrifying. But Daniel saw nothing of it, being more concerned with saving his own skin.

The black stood still, watching as the gipsy finally disappeared. They heard the noise of the horse being slapped and kicked, then the beating of hooves on the road, rushing away towards distant Hertford.

As John Ferris finally moved, conscious that he had been holding his breath for an unconscionably long time, the figure came and knelt beside him.

'Brutus York,' sighed John. 'By Mary and Joseph you are right welcome friend.'

The negro smiled at him. And John felt no shame at all when he realised that he had tears streaking down his cheeks.

CHAPTER EIGHT

'That hart, dear heart, foreswore the heart's own deer.'

The sun came pouring down from an unseasonably warm autumn sky, not a single cloud sullying the dome of unspoilt blue. There was a small crowd of around thirty souls lolling around the makeshift stage on the back of the troupe's battered hay-wagon.

> 'Wherein the great leviathan sunders no more
> unto the cleaved main,
> No more may I, lest she return again.'

There was a smattering of tardy applause, the clapping of chopped hands ringing across the narrow strip of village green.

The play that they were performing was called 'The Spavined Swain', and was written, originally, by a little-known dramatist called Blind Angus Weldon, the infant phenomenon from Peebles in Scotland. But it had been considerably abbreviated and altered by the manager of the touring company, Caleb Thorn. Caleb was lurching towards his sixtieth year, accompanied thither by copious drafts of good ale which tended to sometimes make the delivery of his speeches a matter of luck rather than judgement.

John Ferris had been with Thorn's company of strolling players for two weeks, since his rescue by Brutus, and had quickly found that he had a certain talent for the thespian arts. Thorn had welcomed him with open arms, delighted to have some new blood with his troupe. Swiftly enlisting him as a player of bit parts in the first couple of days, promoting him to the leading roles when their senior actor was unlucky enough to be caught in the hen-house of the local magistrate of a town a few miles back. With the wife of that same local magistrate.

Now it was time for the great sword-fight. Himself, playing John McCampbell, battling with lath claymores against Thorn himself as the evil Baron Dougal MacDougall of the Clan MacDougall. While the object of their passion, Fiona the beggar-maid of the glen, stood tied to a rickety pole at the rear of the tiny stage, occasionally making her presence felt with a feeble scream.

'Thou sturdy knave.'

'What sayest thou?'

'I say that thy breath is that of dogs and that thy pizzle is that of a squeaking mouse.'

Thorn drew back as though struck, clapping a hand to his furrowed brow. This sometimes meant that he had quite lost the thread of his own lines and needed assistance so John readied himself with a prompt.

But all was well. 'Thou arrant fool. Know not that I am the blest babe . . . I meant the best blade, in all of Fife and the kingdoms and earldoms of the South.'

It should have been 'North', but John had

become used to Caleb's frequent departures from their prepared text.

'Lay on MacDougall of MacDougall, and curs'd be he that first shall call for rest.'

They began to battle with careful, exaggerated movements, bringing howls of laughter from the crowd. Some supporting John and some Caleb, filling their laughter with advice and encouragement. Much of it exceedingly bawdy and crude.

A turnip sailed through the air, striking Caleb on the shoulder, putting him off balance and nearly sending him staggering off the back of the wagon. Behind a torn curtain John saw that Brutus was grinning widely, his mouth wrapped around a half loaf and some salted beef.

'What cur tossed that?' he asked, departing from character, and facing the villagers, his false moustache bristling with anger.

'I am Richard, from the hamlet of Billericay, and I threw the turnip,' replied a tiny, wizened man with a halt leg.

Caleb sniffed. 'I shall waste no breath on such a lame rogue,' he said. Turning to John again and aiming a mighty blow at him with his wooden sword.

'Oh, help me, gentle sir,' called Fiona. Played by a London wench named Betty Barrell. A lively girl of eighteen with a merry smile and a tongue that could take the skin off a man with its invective better than a carter's lash.

'Caitiff,' sneered John, curling his lip as well as he could.

'Aye, and marry and will,' riposted Caleb. It was one of his meaningless lines that he often threw in at such times, when the genuine dialogue had briefly slipped his mind.

'And to the death.'

'So be it.'

'Die cursed MacDougall of MacDougall,' shouted John, thrusting his sword carefully between Caleb's chest and arm. Enjoying the cheers from the crowd.

There were occasions when Caleb Thorn would milk his dying scenes for all they were worth. Dragging them out interminably until it seemed he was determined never to die at all.

But it had been a long day's drive and the sun was still high in the sky. If they were speedy in their collection from the crowd and didn't linger over their midday meal, then they might manage to fit in a second performance before evening drew their final curtain.

To John's relief it was a scant minute of two 'ere the convulsions and eye-rolling ended and the body, after a couple of last twitches, became still. Then all that was needful was to release the virtuous maiden from her plight, ignoring her wanton whispering in his ear. Mouth a few platitudes and then it was time for the final speech. Waving his sword in a generous gesture towards the curtain where the flower of Scotland's chivalry was supposedly concealed.

'Come nobles all, and let's away,
To test the fortunes of some happier day!'

The applause rippled and he disappeared behind the curtain, reappearing with Betty Barrell, to be joined by Caleb and by Brutus and the other members of the raggle-taggle company.

'Quick, out with the basket 'ere they all slip off to the alehouse,' hissed Caleb out of the corner of his mouth, meanwhile bowing low and long as if the peasants were the finest audience he had ever had the honour of playing before.

The collection was a good one. Fifteen shillings, four pence, three farthings and two buttons. The best in the previous week.

In the end Caleb decided that they wouldn't bother to move on that afternoon. This decision was prompted partly by one of the local gentry requesting them to put on a second performance of a different play at five that evening. And partly by the colossal amounts of ale that he had consumed with his meal of meat and pickles.

While he slept it off John decided that he would go quietly among the trees and rest. Much as he was relishing the life of a strolling player, and the companionship of the group, it was tiring. And his ordeal at the hands of Robert Monk had left him weaker than he had thought.

He carried a stone jar of local cider, munching the last of a brace of fine apples, stored from the summer, the fresh taste of the sun on his lips. Brutus walked a short way with him, then turning back.

'I needs must read the words if we are to play the Moor this even,' he said.

Their version of the Bard's 'Othello' was somewhat shorter than the original. Consisting of only four characters and seven scenes. And, if the truth be told, the Caleb Thorn version of the great drama had suffered some radical changes, shifting it from tragedy to bawdry. With much word-play on the size of the negro's sexual member, for which Brutus was well-suited. John was Iago, played as a London bully who was pimping for Desdemona, played by Miss Barrell. And Caleb himself had lifted the character of Polonius and transmuted it to a rustic gravedigger who kept appearing and commenting on the action.

With a wealth of gesture that generally went down very well with their rural audiences.

John watched his friend vanish towards the three wagons that they used in their travels. Seeing the broad back, muscles rippling beneath the thin white shirt. Reflecting on how lucky he was to have such a loyal and true comrade.

With the help of the black all things were possible and Monk and his minions had best guard their very shadows against attack.

But it was not yet time for that.

He found a quiet place, near a mill-stream, the wooden wheel creaking around, water splashing into a sun-dappled pool. It was the first time that John had been able to sit down and feel at peace with the world for many a long day. For the first time he even wondered whether this vengeful quest of his was truly worth the pain of the travel. What mattered it to him whether Monk rode free across the bloody land, burning and torturing as he went? John knew right well that there was scant hope of ever recovering the money stolen. And revenge would do naught to bring back the lives of his parents.

But there was . . .

'Mary,' he said, eyes locked to the tumbling waters. 'Mary.'

'Nay, lad. It be Betty,' came the voice from behind him.

He looked round, hand dropping automatically to the hilt of his sword. But it was not there. One of the few rules that Thorn ever pressed was that none of his company should ever wear a sword or pistol. Knowing from bitter experience that players were often fond of their ale, and were also prone to trouble from local rowdies. It was all too easy to stick a rapier through the belly of some teasing yokel and then find yourself dangling from the gibbet before the day was out.

So John's sword and his Ripoll pistol both rested in the wagon he shared with Brutus and two other men, Benjamin and Francis.

'Why, cully,' she laughed. 'I vow your eyes seek some demon.'

John smiled at her perception. 'Indeed, there are those who wish me ill.'

'I know, lad. Brutus told us somethin' of the witchfinder and your chase of him.'

'Aye. Yet, I was but thinking of Monk.'

'And your Mary?'

He nodded. 'Yes.'

'She is pretty?'

He nodded once more. Pointing to the grass at his side, brushing away some of the first dead leaves of the autumn for her to sit by him. The actress did so, folding her legs elegantly beneath her.

'She is, Betty. By Mary and Joseph, but she is!'

The girl stretched out, closing her eyes. 'By the

wounds of Jesus on the Cross, John, but this weather is most wonderful. I have known years with Caleb when we have been locked in some poxin' barn in Blackfriars with barely three-ha'pence and a dose of the clap between us all.'

He looked down at her, comparing her in his mind's eye with Mary Villers. Seeing the similarities and also the differences.

Both had blonde hair. But Mary's was the fine delicate yellow of wheat seen through a summer haze. Betty's was a brighter yellow. Somehow, cheaper. Like the difference between silver and pinchbeck.

Mary's eyes were blue as blue. John had once seen a painting of the Mediterranean sea, by a man who swore that the colours were utterly true to life. That was the blue he recalled from the eyes of his beloved Mary Villers.

Betty opened her eyes, grinning impishly up at him. And he saw that they were also blue. But it was a paler blue. More the colour of the sky when rain threatened and the wind was in the east. And they were somewhat pink where they should have been white.

At a distance Betty's skin was clear and fresh, like a child. But close up he knew how coarse it was, spoiled and blighted by the paints and unguents that she applied for the stage. There were narrow lines etched deep around her nose and mouth.

Mary was different.

Different as there is a difference between the gods and the mortals.

'Give you a farthing for your thoughts, Master Ferris,' she said.

'I thought of how lucky I had been that Brutus had found me as he did.'

'It was some tinker, was it not? Shifty little cove. Brought word you was after Monk and in some hardship.'

'Aye. It is passing strange, but had it not been for Orlando Logbane I should never have known what Monk intended. Had it not been for his betrayal they would not have caught me as they did.'

'And had it not been for his message to the black then . . .'

'Then I should have been most cruelly tortured. Whipped and racked and scourged. Burned and pricked with needles of fire. Cut and . . . Oh, dealt with in a most wicked and unjust manner.'

She rolled over half on her side and he noticed that the bodice of her brown dress was unlaced, showing the soft swell at the top of her bubbies.

'And by this day you would have been done to death, John. And a waste of a fine, bonny man.'

'Aye. Burned in the fires or, mayhap, drowned in deep water. Or hanged. Monk has many strings to his bow and can use them all right well.'

Her hand was on him, crabbing its way down over his arm, onto his chest. Spidering its way lower.

'And all of this flesh would be rottin' on some lonely crossed-road gallows in chains.'

'Food for crows, sweet maid,' he replied. Feeling that he ought to stop her movement, but finding it pleasant, her fingers warm on his stomach as she burrowed beneath his cambric shirt.

'Aye, such food as is meat for crows. Most like

the watery orbs that shine beneath the caves of the furrowed skull.'

It was a line from a play that they had been performing only the previous day. John grinned at the wanton girl.

'But sure those eyes behold a softer light than that harsh iron that binds my heart.'

The play was adapted by Caleb Thorn from some earlier epic. Now it ran for six scenes and contained three rapes and two suicides. It was entitled 'The Sailor's Return'.

'Johnny, lad . . .' she whispered, delving beneath the broad leather belt that encircled his waist.

He looked about him. The wheel kept up its steady rhythm, pounding round and round, the water streaming from it, bubbling and dancing. The woods around were quiet, seeming empty. The village was a good half mile away, to the west.

Betty was a fanciable enough jade, and it had been long. So long since he had lain with Mary. He felt himself reacting to her touch.

'Ah, there he comes, Johnny. Comes to my calling like a gudgeoned trout.'

She took his hand, unprotesting, drawing it to her. Pressing it to her breast. Sighing at his touch. He found himself stroking her skin. Pushing his hand further into the bodice until his finger and thumb cupped her nipple. It hardened against the palm of his hand like a tiny animal.

'Yes, lad. Yes . . .'

She gripped him tight, rubbing her hand up and down the erect shaft of his penis. For a moment of blanking panic he thought that he was going to spend against her fingers, so long had it been. But he recovered himself and his control, rolling half on his side so that he could kiss her, tasting the faint flavour of the paint and makeup on her lips. Her mouth opened and sucked his tongue in, nipping at him with her feral teeth.

The pressure on him increased, the movement faster. Her breath warm in his ear.

'I have no underpinnings on, Johnny. I am wet and heated for your touch. Come, release your ten troopers to storm my citadel.'

'My engine will batter at the ramparts, Madam,' he whispered. Further lines from 'The Sailor's Return'.

'Yes, oh yes. Come take me, lover.'

Her fingers were more insistent. No man on earth could have resisted such blandishment. Even the most austere saint on the calendar would have fallen for Betty Barrell.

Or risen for her.

Within a hundred beats of his heart John Ferris had allowed all of his resolutions to slide away from him. He had sworn that he would remain faithful to his dear, sweet Mary Villers. Not even think of lying with another woman, let alone this eighteen-year-old London doxy.

Betty was on her back, skirts hoisted, and he was on top of her, his breeches unlaced and drawn down about his ankles. John was kneeling between her spread thighs, readying himself, her hand still holding him. Guiding him.

He lowered himself on her, ready to drive himself into her. Wanting her now with a desire that bordered on blind lust.

When they both heard the voice.

Muffled by the churning of the big wheel, slapping at the mill-stream.

'Johnny! Betty, my dove.'

'It's Caleb,' he hissed, eyes screwed tight with his anger.

'Fuck 'im. Let him come,' she said, still trying to draw him into her.

'Time to get ready for the show, children. The hour has struck and the crow has . . . crowed.' He wasn't far away.

'Please, Johnny . . .'

But the moment had passed and they both knew it.

Away to the west the sky was reddening with the promise of a fine tomorrow.

CHAPTER NINE

The promise of the sky had been more than kept.

It was another wonderful day. As they had moved slowly along through the baking land, the sun had scorched down like molten brass. There was not the slightest hint of any wind. No cloud to mar the perfection of the sky.

John was walking along the leading cart, the horse patiently clopping at his side. It had been a great relief to him that the Mendozas had kept Morgana tethered to the same wagon that had been his prison. Brutus had been able to liberate both animal and master at one and the same time.

Now the raw-boned, hard-mouthed bay mare was tied to the back of the last of the troupe's carts. Where even she would find it difficult to either bite or kick anyone.

Brutus drove the first cart, Betty dozing over the reins of the second horse. Francis and Benjamin sat together on the seat of the last of the carts, engrossed in close conversation.

At first John had simply thought them the best of friends. But their sleeping arrangements, in the same wagon, beneath the same blankets, made him realise that it was something more than friendship.

Dust came up from the heels of the men, the

hooves of the horses, hanging behind the three carts in a shimmering grey curtain. Caleb was in an expansive mood, amusing John with his endless anecdotes about life on the road. Of cheated landlords and cheating actors. Of foul weather and of fair friends. Of drink and women and jealousy and of violence done and received.

And of the War.

'It has harmed us, Johnny, lad.'

'Harmed? How? By killing off those who would come to watch and pay?'

Caleb nodded. He was a stout man, his cheeks lined with a network of purple veins. His nose was swollen and red, less inflamed than when he was in drink, but still seeming bright enough to light their way on the darkest night.

'No silver.'

'No.'

'And precious little copper when the soldiers have come this way.'

'They are for the Parliament in these parts, are they not?'

'Aye. There has been great sorrow from the rough troopers of the King. It has left a cup that doth brim with bitterness, wormwood and with gall.'

'Cavaliers. Aye, I have seen some of their handiwork about the country.'

'You see it as it happens, Johnny. I have come by weeks after and still seen the fresh scars on faces. The tears in eyes. Burn marks upon walls and pens where no cattle feed.'

'I have seen much of this.'

Unconsciously he was rubbing at his injured

elbow, thinking back to the bloody days of the fighting. Relieved in many ways that he no longer needed to be a part of such deeds.

'The place we go to, John.'

'It is close?'

'Aye. An hour. Less.'

'Its name?'

'Greenwood End.'

'Large?'

'A hundred souls. There was trouble here, I heard, some months back.'

'The King's men, Caleb?'

The older man nodded. 'Aye. I heard of a torn girl, found trembling by a local stream. Of some men who were taken and returned gelded. And of some that did not return at all.'

It was a familiar enough tale. One that John had heard during the last long months that he had been pursuing Robert Monk. And he had seen the deep hatred that it produced, on both sides of the conflict.

'Should we go on to their hamlet, Caleb?'

'Why not? If they have even a few coppers, then it is coppers for us. And if they do not, then it is truly a poor place that will not feed good players such as ourselves.'

John walked on a few paces in silence. 'Are there soldiers still about these woods?'

The older man sniffed. Sniffed once more, with greater vigour. Hawking up phlegm and spitting it out into the dusty hedgerow.

'There always be soldiers, Johnny Ferris. Always. Hidin' and lurkin' about the place as if they owned this poor land. This royal throne of kings, this sceptered isle. This . . . But I must not go on.'

A pigeon startled both men as it burst flapping from a clump of beeches, the trees resplendent in their red and brown finery.

'Mary and Joseph!' exclaimed John, stopping in his tracks and looking around him.

'It be but a tiny bird, most lovely of God's creatures,' said Thorn, smiling. 'Draw not thy sword, sweet coz.'

John didn't respond. 'When a bird flies with such speed, then some thing or man has frighted it.'

The voice came from the beeches, loud and strong. 'Truly said, brethren. Move one hair on yer heads and you are dead men.'

CHAPTER TEN

They were practically ready to begin their play. 'The Sailor's Return'. Six scenes and a whole pot of their fake blood ready behind the fluttering curtain.

John had his false beard glued in place, a threadbare wig netted over his own long hair. He played Thomas, the errant son of a once-great family. Who had gone away to sea as a child and had been marooned by his wicked uncle. But he had returned with his trusty black companion to try and reclaim his birthright from the evil relation and also bring aid to his betrothed Ruth.

In the original play much of the action had taken place on board a sailing schooner. Upon a desert island to the south of Africa. In the palace of the omnipotent Akond of Boaz. The harem of the same. The dungeons of the same. A fortress in Moldavia. And finally back to the humble cottage of Mistress Ruth.

In Caleb Thorn's version of the drama all of the early action was told in one hasty recitation that Betty Barrell kept forgetting. And the whole six scenes were set in the humble cottage.

'You are sure you have the bag of blood, John?' hissed Brutus.

'Indeed. Here in my chest, ready to burst as soon as I prick it with this bodkin.'

'Without the blood this performance will be naught. And now that the good folk of Greenwood End are once more our friends . . .'

Thorn was right.

The voice from the beech thicket had promised a speedy end to anyone who crossed them. John had been tempted to go for Morgana and spur his way out of the danger. Guessing that the road behind would still be clear of the ambush. Also trusting that the peasants who had snared them would be poor shots at any distance.

But he turned and saw Brutus, half-standing, jaw dropping at the speed of the ambuscade. And he recalled in that fraction of frozen time how the black had travelled night and day across country, merely to try and save the life of a comrade. It would have been churlish to have run at that moment.

So he had stood, stricken, waiting what the fates had to offer.

The leader of the villagers had been a tall, stout man, a little into his thirties, with a beard of raven black. His hair was also of a midnight hue, but with a streak of silver running through it as though a sword blade had been laid across his pate. His name was Hawes. Jonathan Hawes.

As the actors stood still in the pathway, taking care to keep their hands well free of any weapons, men came pouring from the thickets. John counted two dozen and seven, but he suspected that any leader worth his salt would have left others behind out of sight.

'Your names?' Hawes had demanded. Listening in silence, muscular arms folded, as they introduced themselves to him. Nodding at each of them, glancing around at others of the village, as if he was seeking some kind of clue or confirmation.

'You have seen any of the King's men about as you travelled these roads? No? They have been here.'

Caleb had spoken up. 'I know of their visit, Master Hawes. Word has been about the country, fast as a winging swift. Of the evil that was done.'

The tall man kept his face still, free of emotion. 'They are back.'

'Soldiers!'

John Ferris felt a touch of concern. The Royalists were sometimes less than kindly towards those who had fought against their cause. Bayonets heated in a fire until they glowed cherry-red, inserted slowly into the rectum was one of their tricks.

'Aye, Master Thorn. We have heard they are riding this way once more.'

'The same company?'

Hawes nodded. 'The same.'

Thorn had swallowed hard, eyes flicking nervously to the empty stretch of road behind them. 'When . . .? That is, how far are . . .?'

'They will be here within three hours.'

Betty Barrell had jumped down from her cart in a flurry of skirts. 'Then let's get soddin' moving, Caleb! Bastard fight's all we need.'

Hawes had shaken his head. 'You are good at

your craft, are you not, Master Thorn? I have seen you twice before. You can render us great assistance.'

John Ferris had stepped forwards. 'If we wish to go on, then you will allow us to leave?'

'Now, I don't know . . .' Hawes had stopped. Staring at John. 'I know thee. I know thee.'

'Be he a Cavalier deserter, Jonathan?' asked one of the men that circled them. Moving closer, hefting a rusty sickle with great purpose.

'I know not if . . . You were a soldier?'

'Aye, Master Hawes. I was.'

'You have run from the fights?'

'If you were to stand alone against me and ask that, friend, then I would deal you a sturdy answer.'

'Such talk comes cheap, Master . . . Ferris, you said was your name. Ferris. Wait, there was a Captain who fought next to us at Gainsborough. Aye, that is . . .'

'It is. I fell from my mare and quite broke my arm. I have not fought since that day.'

Hawes shook his hand, vigorously, revealing a strength beyond even his great size. John thought in passing that his angry challenge to the villager might have been proven rash had it come to exchanging a buffet or two.

'Then you can help us, Captain, can you not? This is the plan.'

Francis and Benjamin were whispering together on the far side of the wagon, trying to ensure that they knew their lines for 'The Sailor's Return' rather better than at their last performance. But both of them kept allowing their attention to wander, peering round the corner of the wagon that was to be their stage.

Peering at their audience.

Mainly peering at the men who sat grouped near the front of the forty or fifty villagers of Greenwood End.

Royalist soldiers.

The cavalry patrol that Hawes had told them was on the way to the hamlet. The self-same soldiers who had raped and pillaged and slain on their previous passing through the district.

They had come cantering in to Greenwood End around the time that the company had nearly finished setting up their stage ready for the production. Caleb Thorn had lost his temper with Hawes, ignoring the villager's greater size and muscle. Ignoring the ring of men around him. Ramming a tubby forefinger into Hawes' leather jerkin, emphasising every point with another poke.

His words had been simple.

'We are players, you great ox-faced fool. Why should we become embroiled in your damned revenge plans?'

'Because if you do not, then we shall slay you, Master Thorn,' the man had replied.

It was a pressing argument.

And so they had agreed a compromise. The troupe would do their play, and they would take no part in whatever might happen. That had been made clear as clear by Thorn, and no manner of threat could change his mind. Hawes had come to John. Telling him how he had been a sergeant in the

Parliamentary forces until a Royalist hanger had opened up his skull and near blinded him. He had appealed to his loyalty to the forces of the right, but John had shaken his head. Reminding Hawes that for him the War was indeed over.

He had gone with Thorn, saying that they would do their play, but they would not fight.

'What ever shall come to pass?' asked Hawes.

'Aye. Whatever shall come to pass.'

There were a round sixteen of the soldiers.

A captain, sergeant and fourteen troopers. John knew the type. Had seen them in half a hundred skirmishes. Knew them. Hated them.

He knew also that there were good men on both sides of the conflict. Men of honour and courtesy. Soldiers who enjoyed the sport of fighting and were honourable towards their enemies.

But they were few and extremely far between.

Far too many were men of little breeding. Men whose idea of a fine battle was to come down upon an inferior and ill-armed force, helpless for them to butcher. Preferably with women and ale to follow, spiced with the torture and slaughter of bound prisoners.

This patrol was of that common herd.

Their captain was in his late twenties. Lean and short, with a hat that sported a brace of partridge feathers, trailing and elegant. His name was Lord Rodney Chartham, and he came from the county of Buckingham. He sported drooping moustaches and his loose jerkin and breeches were trimmed with some draggled lace.

His men were a hard-eyed crew, heavily-armed, sitting in groups close to the front. Their swords resting in their scabbards on the grass at their sides. It was noticeable that the majority of the younger men of Greenwood End had vanished as soon as their scouts brought word that the patrol was nearly upon them.

The women of the community moved among the soldiers, offering them mugs of ale, and bread and cheese. John and the rest of the actors were busy about their preparations. Caleb passed by each of them hissing out the warning that they must not become involved, whatever happens.

'Stay on stage, hearties all. Go not from it and all will be well.'

'What do the good folk intend, Caleb?' asked Benjamin.

'I know not and I care not, lad. That way lies a safety of a kind.'

The light was fading away as they began their play.

John Ferris wasn't on stage at the beginning and he sat quietly behind the curtain, watching the bright rays of the setting sun as they came darting through the gaps. Tiny motes of dust, golden in the sun, climbed towards the heat. Seeming to John like some fanciful portrayal of the blessed souls mounting to Paradise in a gentle host.

He could hear the rich, fruity tones of Caleb Thorn as the Chorus who introduced all the bloody action in the play.

'Good gentles all, thrice welcome to this stage,
Where plays shall show the sides of joy and rage,

And all men love the deeds of courage bold,
Where maids are wooed and won, and legends
told.'

A ripple of polite applause, and a resounding belch that John guessed was from one of the soldiers. Caleb appeared at the back of the wagon, motioning for Betty and for Brutus to get out and begin their first scene.

'Those curs mean trouble, lad,' he said. 'They have near drunk the place dry and an hour and a half of this still to go.'

John was puzzled by the interest that Jonathan Hawes had shown in their play. Quizzing him closely on how the action went. Asking him which were the most dramatic moments. Where came the killings. The screams.

The climactic scene was where Betty was ravished by Brutus while John stood at the side of the stage and watched. Supposedly with his brains addled by a blow. Then, at a line and a scream from Betty he was to run on stage and spit the black, receiving a grave wound himself.

Hawes had asked him what the cue-line was. Making him repeat it three times to make sure that he had it in his mind.

'Spare me thy heathen blade!!'

During his short weeks with the company, John Ferris had already encountered several difficult audiences. Some that had been bored, some drunk, and one or two that had been actively hostile. But Captain Chartham and his men succeeded in combining all three attributes. By the time the penultimate scene had begun nearly half of the soldiers were asleep or comatose. The rest were making things difficult for whoever happened to be on the stage at that moment. Calling out and whooping. Impersonating animals and throwing empty beakers. Picking up hunks of bread or apples and heaving them at the actors.

The women of Greenwood End still did their best to please the Royalists. Ignoring the groping and the crude jests. But it was obvious to John as he watched from behind his false whiskers that there was a thin line between the jests and the reality. If the ale continued to flow for many minutes longer some of the troopers would be grabbing at the girls with real purpose.

The only men there were either lads below the age of fourteen, or doddering old fellows past fifty. Yet none of the cavalrymen seemed to notice the lack of the village's menfolk. Carrying on with their drinking, barely bothering to watch or listen to the play.

The setting sun touched lightly on the audience. Glittering off the long-bladed knives that all of the women carried tucked into their aprons to cut the bread and the cheese for their unwelcome visitors.

The wife of Hawes was a stately woman, sailing among the ribald Cavaliers with an air of supreme indifference. She, more than any other, seemed to be concentrating on the play. Listening closely to each line as if it might have some special meaning for her.

John Ferris began to suspect what was to happen, but he kept his own council.

Betty Barrell was stretched across the bench that

served as a bed, her bodice torn discreetly open, showing the tops of her breasts – bringing the greatest cheers of the performance. Brutus York, in a great cuirass of painted tin, was miming the opening of his breeches, waving a mighty scimitar about his head. Acting with much rolling of eyes.

Watching him, John realised how much he had come to love the tall negro.

'Nay, nay,' shrieked the girl. 'Spare me thy heathen blade!'

The laughter was drowned in screams.

And much blood flowed. Real blood.

CHAPTER ELEVEN

'Spare me thy heathen blade.'

John Ferris was just moving from the side of the wagon to respond to Betty's theatrical cry for help when he caught movement from the corner of his eye. Turning to face the audience.

Seeing.

Seeing Jocasta Hawes, kneeling behind the pig-faced sergeant of the Royalist cavalry who had been trying to paw at her legs. Seeing the thin-blade of her carving-knife as it sliced through the side of the man's neck, opening up the massive artery that pulsed beneath his right ear.

Seeing blood, fountaining high in the air, catching the last rays of the sun, bright crimson.

Hearing the man start to cry out in pain and horror. Hearing Jocasta's ringing scream. 'Now!! Now, at 'em, all!! At 'em!!!'

Knives flashing all through the audience as the girls and women went for their selected victims. Sometimes two of them to one soldier. Slitting throats. Opening up bellies. Hacking savagely at unprotected groins. Cutting great gobbets of living flesh from the faces of sleeping men.

'Mary and Joseph,' whispered John Ferris, stopping stricken, in mid-stride. The others all checking what they'd been doing and watching the fight.

Not truly a fight.

The massacre.

John watched as at least ten of the Royalists were slaughtered by the women. Some sleeping, some so drunk that they barely knew what was happening. Some sliding from this world to the next in ignorance of their own passing, aware only of sharp pain for a fleeting moment or two, and of warmth and of wetness about their bodies.

But not all were so easily taken.

Four, no, five, including the Captain and the beefy Sergeant, were up, pushing off the clawing women. Managing to draw their own swords.

'It will be a shambles, Johnny,' said Brutus York, appearing beside Ferris.

'We swore to keep our hands empty, friend,' he replied.

'Where be their men?' asked Betty Barrell, standing like a rabbit before a ferret, paralysed by the horror of the scenes around them.

'There,' called Caleb Thorn, pointing to the nearest fringe of woodland, where a couple of dozen men of Greenwood End came running to aid their women-folk.

'Too late for some,' said John.

Captain Chartham aimed a ferocious blow at the wife of Jonathan Hawes, opening up a cut along the top of her right shoulder. Fortunately for her the soldier was off balance, eyes wide with rage and with shock. Another woman lunged at him from behind, her thin knife breaking as it glanced off his belt. Immediately the Cavalier was round on her, with the ferocity of a trapped mongrel. Using the pommel of his sword to knock her to the ground, then spitting her with the point. The blow so savage that the wretched woman was pinned to the dry earth, wriggling and kicking, her hands bleeding as she tried to pull herself up and off the blade.

In the midst of that carnage, Ferris heard the officer laugh. Laugh at the dying woman, with death all around him.

'Men'll finish 'em off,' hissed Benjamin, one hand resting on the arm of his friend, Francis.

The ambush had been nearly perfect. But Hawes had not allowed for the scant seconds that it took him and the remainder of the men of the hamlet to break from cover and aid their wives and daughters.

The cavalry patrol were hardened soldiers, used to skirmish and bitter fighting. Even in that few seconds, despite their initial crippling losses, they wrought a fearsome revenge on the village.

John saw at least a dozen women go down in that brief time. All dead or dying or grievously mutilated.

There were still four of the patrol standing, grouped together now, swords all drawn and scarlet. Chartham, the Sergeant and two middle-aged troopers. Cutting a scything path of destruction as they began to move fast towards the side of the village where their horses were tethered.

'They will 'scape!' called John, unable to contain himself. Pointing to the animals, trying to attract the attention of Hawes himself.

But the leader of the community was more intent in rescuing his wife, who was down on the blood-slick earth, fending off a sabre blow from one of the troopers. His power and strength were so much greater than hers, and his great blade came screaming down. Shattering her frail knife, carrying on down and through.

'Jesus and the Cross!' exclaimed Betty Barrell, looking away.

The sword cut the woman's right hand off at the wrist. The force sending it skittering across the cropped turf towards the actors' wagons. The fingers were still clenched around the hilt of the broken knife, and threads of skin and tendon trailed ragged after it.

A musket boomed, obscuring the scene for a moment behind a cloud of powder smoke. As the wind cleared it they all saw the soldier who had maimed Jocasta Hawes, rolling on his back, hands clutching his face. Trying to stem the blood that poured between his fingers.

Another man, the Sergeant, fell under a hail of swinging blows from two of the younger men, both armed with hand-sickles. They cut the soldier apart, hacking off his left arm close to the shoulder. One of them stooping and ripping apart the delicate knee-joint, bringing the Royalist screaming to the dirt, where they continued to hack at him. Twice cutting each other in their eagerness to finish the wretch.

Brutus pointed to the left. Where a lad in his late teens was hefting a long-handled pitchfork. Balancing it as if it were a javelin and he a Roman mercenary.

'Yes,' whispered John, not even aware that he had spoken.

Seeing the weapon hiss towards its target. Striking the last of the common soldiers through the lower back. The impact knocking him on his face among a group of howling women.

They were on him like terriers on a fleeing rat. The King's man disappeared under them, and there was one single, muffled yelp of agony. Then there was only the snarling of the women. Knives glittering in the last rays of the day's sun. Rags of clothes were hurled from the mob, and then a tall young girl stood upright. Mouth open with excitement. Her dress torn, showing her breasts, stained with splattered blood. In her upraised hands, like some Greek goddess of savage revenge, she held the trooper's severed genitals.

'Blessed Virgin, spare us all!' said Francis, clasping his friend to his chest, burying his face against him so that he need not see more.

Hawes was first to close on the officer, now the sole survivor from the patrol. But his plight was not so desperate as might have appeared. Chartham had only one wounded woman between him and the horses, only forty paces or so from the stage where Ferris stood with the others. His sword was still safe in his fist, and he was unscathed.

'If he is free then our lives are forfeit,' said Thorn. 'He will bring others and name us as party to this killing.'

John hadn't even considered that, but it was clearly true. An entire patrol being wiped away as cleanly as this might have awesome repercussions. Greenwood End would do well to escape a further penalty for their actions. And the company could well be dragged down to perdition with them.

'Stand, bastard!' roared Hawes, waving his sickle at the soldier.

Who paused in his flight, turning to face the rushing peasant. Chartham smiled. 'Come to me, filth. And I shall end . . .'

Cutting in a sideways slashing blow that Hawes just managed to parry. But the second thrust was too much and the villager dropped, holding his side where the keen sword had sliced through his jerkin, opening up a long wound across his ribs.

Lord Rodney Chartham was smiling, lips curled in his madness. Nobody now stood between him and his horse. Given a fair start he knew that his grey stallion would outrun anything these dung-eaters could put against him.

One last blow to kill this mewling rogue at his feet. Then away. With the prospect of a bloody revenge against this place.

'Not one stone on another,' he shrieked, hefting the blade for the killing thrust.

'No!' shouted John Ferris, leaping cat-footed from the back of the wagon, forgetting that he still wore his stage wig and everything needful for his part in the play.

'How?' said the Cavalier, spinning on his heel, seeing a wild-eyed, bewhiskered madman running at him, waving a sword that was clearly made of wood.

'Nay, Master . . .' called Hawes, struggling to try and get away from the soldier.

John Ferris was never the sort of man to hazard his own life on some utterly lost and hopeless charge. But if there was a chance of living, then he would take it.

And if he could also aid another, then so be it.

Despite his ineffectual weapon, his speed and daring were greatly on his side. Leaping in at the bewildered Royalist, waving the wooden sabre. Seeing Chartham begin the blow that would cleave him from pate to belly.

Diving forwards as if he was about to enter shallow water, twisting like a pike as he did so. Using the wooden sword to hit out at the man's legs. Hitting him just above the top of his muddied riding-boots. Chartham was thrown a little off balance by the attack, cursing at the pain of the blow. As John came up into a crouch, Chartham spat at him. Seeing his path to the horses blocked by this bearded actor.

'Damn you for a bastard fool,' he said. 'Stand and let me run you through.'

'I am no helpless wench, you Royalist cur,' replied Ferris.

Chartham took a couple of limping steps towards him, the sabre waving at the air in front of him like the tongue of a poisonous reptile.

The wooden blade hadn't the strength to parry a full cut from the sabre, but it was adequate to turn a stroke aside. That was John's plan.

Feinting an attack, and shifting sideways at the last moment. Allowing the Captain to strike at him, angling his body to one side to make sure that the sabre missed him.

It had been a long time since John had engaged in fencing, and the reflexes had lost something of their keen edge. And Chartham's reflexes were sharpened by the adrenalin that pours out with extreme fear.

The sword caught him across the left side of the chest, opening up his woollen jerkin, and the shirt beneath.

'Tapped the claret, you fucker!' grunted Chartham, standing back a pace and drawing breath. Enjoying the result of his skill.

John heard someone screaming, over the general hubbub and noise. Betty Barrell he guessed. And a roar of anger that could only be Brutus York.

Both of them horrified at the sudden spurting of blood from his chest. A great gouting flood of crimson, bright in the evening sun. Spurting from the cut, pattering on the ground near his feet, soaking over his stomach and thighs. Enough blood and more to convince anyone that his wound must be mortal.

'I shall end you,' hissed the soldier.

In parrying the blow with the sabre as it came ripping in at him, John's wooden sword had been broken. So that he now held only a short stump of jagged, sharp, splintered wood. Less than a foot and a half long.

It was enough.

Moving with paralysing speed, considering the bloody wound in his chest, John hurled himself at the Cavalier. Jabbing at the startled man's gaping face, brushing aside the feeble attempt to stop him with the sabre. The sharp piece of wood was like a crude dagger, tearing into Chartham's face. At the last split moment the Royalist tried to turn his head away, so that the blow went through his cheek. Tearing the flesh open, smashing teeth at the angle of his jaw.

The sword dropped from his fingers and he fell,

John on top of him, beginning to scream. The wooden knife rose and fell again, almost taking the soldier's left eye from its socket. Again and again John stabbed at him, using all of his power. Seeing blood spurt, mingling with the flow from his own chest wound.

The wood splintered and broke, this time leaving only a short stump, useless for killing. John Ferris discarded it, seizing the wriggling man by his throat. Locking his fingers at the back of the neck. Thumbs gouging into the gristle of the windpipe. Cutting off the the air from the lungs. Tighter. Squeezing so that Chartham's body stiffened as he tried to throw him off. The man's eyes were breaking from their sockets and the tongue protruded.

Blackening, and swollen. Breath rattled and he tightened his grip, holding the King's man still with his knees on either side of his chest. Leaning down with all of his weight.

'It's done, John,' said Brutus, tapping him on the shoulder.

Ferris had closed his own eyes, concentrating all of his energy on killing the officer. Now he opened them, blinking away sweat. Seeing that Chartham was quite still, head back, mouth open in a rictus of mortal pain.

'Aye, it's done, friend,' he replied.

Betty and Caleb and the rest realised almost at once how he had managed to battle on when there was such a ghastly wound at the centre of his chest, still seeping blood. But the villagers were baffled by it. Baffled until John opened the front of his torn jerkin and showed the small pouch, slit across the centre, leaking with carefully mixed red dye. Thick to look like blood. Good enough to convince even a soldier like Captain Chartham, late of the Royalist forces.

'We shall burn the corpses in a great fire. Break the ashes and bones down to a dust. And spill the remains into the mill-stream. It will be as though they had never been.'

John and the rest nodded at the words of Jonathan Hawes. The elder of the village was standing in the dawn light, by their wagons.

'It was worth it? The game was worth the candle?' asked Caleb Thorn.

'Sixteen of them slain. We lost five. All women. I was not speedy enow in comin' to their aid.'

'A score settled,' said John.

'Aye, Master Ferris. But now there is a debt 'twixt thee and me. I owe you a life.'

John shook his head. 'No, friend. There is no debt. You have settled with the men who near destroyed your lives. I am honoured to be a part of that settling.'

'Then the Lord go with you, John Ferris. And with all of you, friends.'

Brutus clicked his tongue at the leading horse and it began to plod away northwards in the opalescent morning. Hawes raised a hand in salute, ringed by the rest of the village. Some of them showing the signs of the fighting, others with faces still stained by tears at their own losses. John sat with Caleb on the second wagon. Francis and

Benjamin with Betty on the final cart.

They rattled away into the stillness, none of them wishing to talk much.

'You will go and leave us, Johnny?' said Caleb after they had ridden a mile or two.

'How did you know?'

The old man grinned, showing his stained and broken teeth. 'I am an aged dog, and new tricks come hard, Johnny. Say that I felt it, and that is enough.'

'I have been happy this last few weeks, Caleb, and that is the truth of it.'

'But . . .'

'But that fight has made me think again of what I must do.'

'Must, lad?'

'Aye. There are things, Master Thorn, that a man is not able to ride around.'

The old actor nodded his understanding. 'And your quest for Monk is one of those things.'

'It is.'

'Mistress Betty will grieve for your leaving us, Johnny.'

'I too shall grieve.'

'Did you swive with her?'

John looked sideways, seeing the twinkle in Thorn's eyes. 'You lecherous whoremonger, Caleb! Nay, I did not. I have kept my troth to Mary as well as I have been able.'

For a moment he blushed at the vile memory of the way he had been used by Liza Hall in that dungeon. But he had been helpless and could not stop her. Truly?

'Will the black go with you?'

'I did not ask him.'

'He will go. He is a loyal and brave heart, John. We shall miss him sadly.'

'When?'

'Soon?'

'Where will you pursue the rogue?'

'He is from my way of the country. I shall seek him about the town of Hertford and to the east.'

'They say that Hopkins is Witchfinder in Suffolk and in the land of Anglia.'

'Aye. They have divided up the land with their evil ways, Caleb.'

'You will take care?'

'I shall try, friend.'

'If there is anything that we can do, all you need do is whistle.'

John nodded. 'I shall keep that in my mind.'

'Just whistle.'

Three more days drifted by and the weather was finally showing signs of breaking. The wind had shifted around to the east, bringing occasional flurries of light rain. The nights had become colder and the troupe were talking about moving into London for the winter. Brutus agreed to accompany John as he set out once more on the road that was signposted with the destination of 'Revenge'.

A sad parting they made of it, at a windmill by a flooded quarry. Betty wept copiously and Francis and Benjamin were also piping their eyes. Caleb gravely shook the hands of both John and Brutus, pressing a gold sovereign into both their fists.

'Fare thee well.'

'And all of you,' said John, feeling emotion threatening to unman him.

'Nothing more,' sighed Caleb.

'No,' agreed John Ferris, preparing to mount Morgana. 'The rest is silence.'

CHAPTER TWELVE

It was the twenty-fourth day of the month of November in the year of Our Lord, sixteen hundred and forty-five.

The day had been iron-grey, the air cold, tasting of salt. Low clouds squatted over the Essex countryside, occasionally releasing a misty drizzle that turned every now and again to sleet. The previous night there had been a scattering of snow, lying against the bare hedgerows, dusting the barren branches of the trees. The temperature was only a couple of degrees above freezing, so that the breath came pluming out from the horses' nostrils and mouths.

'Snow on Kate's eve, old women shall grieve.'

'What?'

The negro repeated the saw, grinning at the look of disbelief on his companion's face. Brutus was muffled to the eyes, a long shawl wrapped about his head. John Ferris had bought a jacket of double-wool and wore that beneath a leather jerkin. His pistol was safely out of the cold and damp, but his sword hung sheathed at his left hip.

'You made it up, friend.'

'Nay. It is true. At that last village the priest blessed me, thinking I was some errant heathen, telling me then that the morrow was the feast day of the Blessed Saint Katherine of Alexandria.'

The black had once been imprisoned in a small town in Scotland and had shared his cell with an addle-pated youth who could not count beyond 'two' yet knew everything that there was to know about the entire calendar of saints. And he had imparted much of that knowledge to Brutus York.

'And the tale of snow bringing grief to the aged?'

York laughed. 'There was something of my own invention in that.'

'Who was this Katherine of Alexandria?'

'They say she was a rich and virtuous virgin. If such ever existed. She adopted the faith of the Christians. Three score wise men were set by the Emperor, whose name 'scapes me, to refute her beliefs. They failed and all were burned alive. Then she was beaten and thrown into some noisesome gaol.'

John blinked and ducked his head as the wind rose and rattled hail against his face. The track they rode was dappled with grey puddles, ice frosting their edges and mud lay thick all about the dreary land.

'Then they did try to break this Kate upon a wheel, which fell asunder, injuring many of the watchers. Ten score of the soldiers swore their belief to the Christian god and were beheaded there and then.'

'Brutus, you stretch my belief in your tale,' warned John.

'I swear this is what that lackbrain lad told me. And he had such facts at the tips of his fingers. This maid was then beheaded and milk came from her veins. Angels carried her off.'

'And all lived happily ever after,' finished Ferris. 'I vow I have never heard such arrant foolery, Brutus.'

'It is your god, not mine, my friend.'

In the weeks that had passed since they had parted company from Caleb Thorn and his troupe, John and Brutus had been travelling with great caution. Trying to sniff out the plans of the witchfinder, Monk, but not wanting to risk their own falling into one of his snares. It was dangerous enough for word to be out against Ferris himself, but the black was even more conspicuous. They had slipped into the pattern of John riding ahead and finding where Monk had been and was going. Then he and Brutus would circle about and try and get ahead of the witchfinder and his gang. But so far they had been unlucky. Missing him as he turned off to deal with some other business.

Yet, this time they were more hopeful.

'There.'

Stark against the setting sun they saw a gibbet. A double gallows with two bodies dangling in their iron chains. Swinging slowly in unison as the wind caught them. For John it was a hideously familiar picture, bringing back the bitter memory of finding his parents, murdered at Monk's bidding, ending on the felons' tree.

A farmer they had passed a mile back had told them that the witches were being sought. 'Scattered like chaff 'fore the cleansing wind,' had been his words.

And there was the mute and inglorious evidence of that scattering.

'If the weather does not break on us, we should be at Maxwell Green by moon-rise.'

They rode on in silence, hunched against the biting wind. Over to their left John saw a hare break cover and limp trembling through the cropped, sodden grass. Ahead of them the track wound its way between small clumps of trees, disappearing and then showing itself again through the mist.

During the last month his thoughts had turned more towards Mary. His brief flirtation with the lively Betty Barrell had brought home to him how much he missed his betrothed. It was only caution, learned by the dreadful experience as a prisoner, that prevented him from riding in with Brutus and snatching her from the side of the witchfinder. And there was still that uneasy feeling in the pit of his stomach. Why had she not tried to escape? Had there truly been no chances for her? And, since she had not, and seemed to be travelling with the party as a compliant guest, what hold did Monk have over her?

The only answer was that Monk knew something of her family. Some member of the Villers clan must have been under suspicion as a wizard and, perhaps, the witchfinder had agreed to spare them if the beautiful Mary kept him company.

There were other questions.

Questions that even in the darkest hours of the night, when the blood flows slowest, John chose not to examine too closely.

* * *

They camped together in a sheltered hollow, within sight of the flickering lights of Maxwell Green. Yellow lamps showing at the windows of the nearest cottages. It was a community of some hundred souls, with several scattered farms in the district. There was an old church, with a tower of flint, and a large manor-house to the east. And, if the gossips were to be believed, it was the home of a thriving coven of witches.

Brutus lit a fire, foraging for dried wood that would burn bright and warm. Also collecting some moss and greener wood to ensure that the fire lasted through the night.

Food was scarce.

John had been able to eke out their shrinking silver by working for eleven days helping break some horses for a middle-aged lady who lived on the fringes of Epping Forest. A lady who had made it clear to him that had he wished there would have been the possibility of a more permanent position with her. And the position would not have been utterly linked with her horses.

Brutus had killed a dog earlier that same day. Not even dismounting from his horse to do so. Hurling his green-handled knife and striking the limping animal through the back of the neck, toppling it twitching in the mud.

Cut up into neat joints and roasted over the fire, wrapped in mud, the dog was delicious. They had some bread left from their first meal of the day and a flask of ale bought from a tavern during the morning.

'I would not have eaten such a creature had it not been for your skill, Brutus,' said John, leaning back on his blanket and watching the sparks from the fire as the wind whirled them away into the chill air.

'One day I shall have you eating a stew of snake, seasoned with pismires.'

John had heard of people like ditch gipsies eating ants and the like, but it would not have occurred to him a year back that one day he might consider such a repast. Even the idea of devouring a dog was only credible after the hardships of campaigning in the War.

'So much has changed,' he said.

'What was that, John?' asked his companion.

'I did not even know I had spoken out loud, Brutus. It was a thought for myself. So much has passed since the beginning of this year and little of it good.'

As he spoke he rubbed at his injured elbow. The recent cold and wet weather had sent daggers of scraping pain into the damaged joint. Each morning he massaged his arm to try and reduce the stiffness, but it seemed to be growing worse.

'Mayhap we can end the year in better style.'

'By slaying Monk and his villeins. And by rescuing my sweet dove,' replied John.

The negro was picking at his teeth with the frayed end of a narrow twig. Spitting into the fire. Suddenly he reached across the space between them and gripped John by the forearm. Looking seriously into his eyes.

'This year has brought me something that I have always wished for. Something that I have lacked ever since I came first to this land of white faces and blue-eyed children.'

'What is that, my friend?'

Brutus laughed quietly. 'That is it, in a word, John.'

'What word?'

'Friend. You call me "friend". And I too share that emotion for you. I have never known such a friend as you, John Ferris.'

The white man laid his hand on top of the black fist. Clasping it firmly. 'I have never known such a friend as you, Brutus York.'

'I had thought that I could leave you to your hunting of Monk,' continued the negro. 'But when that tinker brought word of your plight, it was as though a skewer had pierced my heart.'

'The debt 'twixt us can never be cleared, Brutus. You know that?'

The black removed his hand. 'Talk to me of owing and of debts and there is an end to all of this, John. I do what I do because of friendship. And for no other reason. It is hurtful to hear you talk this way.'

'I beg pardon, Brutus.'

'No more of debts.'

John smiled. 'No more, my true heart. When once the earth is cleansed of Monk and his scum then you and I . . . and Mary, can find some new life.'

'Together?'

'Aye. Aye, together. If there should be aught left of my inheritance, which I truly doubt, then there will be ample for us to purchase a small farm in some distant part of the land. A part not tainted by Monk's bloody shadow.'

'I would take that kindly, John. To sit with you

and your wife and, perhaps, children. Upon a summer's eve, with the scent of herbs and flowers. I believe that a man could choose a worse time and place to die than in the company of gentle friends. It has always been my hope that one . . .'

The sentence trailed away and John Ferris allowed the quiet moment to remain between them.

The next morning Brutus York insisted that he should go into Maxwell Green alone to try and find out news of Robert Monk.

By sunset he was dead.

CHAPTER THIRTEEN

He had been opposed to it from the start. Preferring to carry out the task of scouting himself. But the black had insisted. Pointing out that Monk had caught him previously under just such a circumstance. Luring him into a village and then snapping shut the jaws of the snare.

It had been snowing once more during the night and John felt unwell. The arm plagued him and he was beginning a cold. Also, he had slept badly and had woken feeling unaccountably depressed. Now that he could see the end of his chase, he somehow wished to postpone matters. To wait until he felt more himself.

It had been a little after eight in the morning when the black had walked away towards the village. Taking care to swaddle himself in layers of heavy clothing, tugging a broad-brimmed hat down over his eyes so that he was virtually invisible within the shadows.

There had not even been a hand-clasp between the two men, but John had watched him disappear into the swirling drizzle.

The agreement had been that Brutus would return as soon as he found news.

The wind was blowing from John Ferris towards

the hamlet, so he would not even have caught the sound of any possible disturbance. There could have been fighting and even muskets used, and he would have heard nothing.

It was a clear possibility that something had gone sadly awry. If Brutus had been caught by Monk, then he would be put to the question. And John knew well that even the strongest of men might weaken and betray what was wanted if Monk and the Mendozas were loosed against him. Should that be the case, then it might only be an hour or so before the dogs were loosed and his camp was discovered.

There was a sullen river winding its way among the trees a furlong or two away from the village, and John decided that it would be as safe a place as any to hide the horses. Leading Brutus's animal and Morgana there, tethering them. Hoping they would make no sound that might bring searchers. The sole benefit of the cold and miserable weather was that there was not likely to be any casual passers-by.

As the morning wore on, the weather seemed to take a marked turn for the worse. The temperature dropped until it was close to freezing. The rain stopped but there were odd flurries of light snow that rattled off the trunks of the trees. John had his pistol tucked into his belt, jerkin fastened loosely so that he could get his hand to the gun if he needed.

As he walked through the dull afternoon towards Maxwell Green he began to hear the sound. A sullen, shifting noise, like an ebbing tide on a shingled beach.

An ugly, animal roaring.

He moved faster, his boot-heels crunching through the thin film of ice that now covered every pool and puddle. His right hand was on the hilt of the sword, slowing him, making him advance at a more cautious, slanting gait.

A road ran through the centre of the village, lined with small wattle and daub cottages. There were two larger houses, each with an attic and dormer windows set into the roof. Each had long gardens and John moved carefully into the nearest one. Past a neat vegetable patch. The rear of the building was shuttered against the cold and smoke came from one of the chimneys. He paused under an aged quince tree, the husks of the summer's fruit still lying neglected in some long grass.

The sound was louder. Cheering, like hounds baying when they sighted their quarry. On an impulse John Ferris drew his sword, feeling the metal cold on his bare fingers. He also reached inside his coat and cocked the pistol, leaving it in his belt.

Snow was beginning to fall with a greater sense of purpose, laying a gentle cover over the harsh, bleak lines of the garden. As he started to walk closer to the house he heard a latch lifting and he moved quickly back into hiding. Seeing an elderly woman appear, looking up at the sky and shivering. Tugging a black shawl over her head and pulling the back door of the house shut behind her. Scurrying around the side and disappearing towards the road.

John looked at the blank shutters, wondering whether someone might be observing him from the cracks between them. Perhaps one of the Mendozas?

But if Brutus York was in the trouble that he suspected then he would be of scant assistance cowering in the rear garden of some old woman's house.

First he must find out what was happening.

It was the sheerest luck that he wasn't caught.

Daniel Mendoza was standing right against the front gate of the house, leaning and talking to a man that John didn't recognise. The gipsy hefted a musket on his right shoulder, swinging a stout cudgel in his hand. The other man held a long pike, its end bent and rusting.

Fortunately, the noise from the street was loud enough to drown the sound of John's feet on the icy ground and he was able to slip back, unseen, into the rear garden of the big house.

If they had guards out, then they must be expecting him, he reasoned. And in that case, then they must have caught poor Brutus. It was vital that he found out where they were holding the black, so that he could begin to plan his rescue. It was obvious that Monk would not miss the chance to try the negro. On the assumption that someone as startling looking would be a prime candidate for suffering under a guilty finding.

But all of that would take time.

If the trial was taking place out of doors, then the obvious location would be on the green. And that must be in front of the house where he sheltered. If he could get in and find his way to a window that overlooked the green, John saw that he would be able to work out how to save the life of the black.

If there was someone within the building, then his life might well be forfeit and his friend would lose all chance of succour.

But, the house was empty.

He walked cautiously in through the kitchen and scullery, past a row of smoked hams hanging from large iron hooks. The door through into the main hallway stood ajar and he pushed it open. Easing it gently as it began to squeak. A tall clock stood ticking to itself near the heavy oak front door. From behind it he could hear the noise of the mob. Muffled, but still swelling. As though their festival was beginning to approach a climax.

If it was Brutus that they were trying, it was puzzling that the noise was ceaseless. It occurred to him that he might be wrong and it could be some other sort of fair or spectacle.

The doors to the rooms on the ground floor were all closed. He tried one, but it resisted him. It was either very stiff, or it was locked.

The light was poor, the bleak afternoon wearing on. John stepped past the clock, to the bottom of the stairs. Pausing and straining his ears. But the house seemed still as death. Silent as the grave.

Quiet as a tomb.

On the first landing he found that all of the doors were also closed, but there was a twisting cupboard staircase that led up to the attics. One at the front overlooking the green and one at the back of the building, the dormer staring blankly out over the large garden.

The front room was filled with lumber. Trunks and old toys. A broken mirror, decorated with golden cherubs holding horns of plenty. A ball-gown, ruffled, its lace gnawed by mice. Spiders had claimed the attic for themselves, their webs so dense that it was difficult to see clear across to the small, leaded window.

But John eventually made it. Moving in with extreme care in case anyone might be looking round and suddenly see his face.

But the crowd of villagers were far too preoccupied to care about him.

They were all facing away from the house. Looking where a group of men were putting the finishing touches to a large fire.

John Ferris knew at that bitter moment that he was too late.

CHAPTER FOURTEEN

John never found out what had happened to lead to his friend's death.

Likely someone saw him and realised that he must be the black that Monk had spoken of. Perhaps a Mendoza. Perhaps Monk himself or the woman. But it didn't matter a damn.

There must have been well over a hundred people packed around the green of the village. The pond stood to one side, fringed with grey ice, already dusted with the falling snow. There were men, with a scattering of women, and several little children, scampering among the feet of the adults.

John immediately made out the trim figure of Robert Monk, directing operations. Pointing here and there with his gloved hands, the two gipsy brothers bustling about to make sure he was obeyed. He couldn't see Liza Hall, and there was no sign of Mary. But he would not have expected her to be present at such a scene. Across the far side of the green he could see that there were lights in some of the windows, and he guessed that there would be others of Maxwell Green watching from the warmth and comfort.

* * *

The next half an hour was the worst of John's entire life. Never had he felt more miserable, more helpless.

More angry.

More alone.

Brutus was stripped of most of his clothing, wearing only a linen shirt, torn across the chest, and stained with blood in two or three places. His breeches were also torn and stained. John could see that the black's hands were tightly bound behind him, straining his shoulders back. A rope ran from his wrists to his neck. The light was not good enough with the snow flurries for John to make out more details. Something glistened at the corner of the negro's mouth, that might well have been blood and his face seemed to be swollen about the eyes.

A torch flared, in the hands of Abraham Mendoza, used to light two others. Monk was saying something and the murmuring faded away, but John could make nothing of it through the closed dormer window. But he guessed that it would be some specious, lying justification for the murder about to be committed. It was some indication of the fear that the witchfinder might be feeling that he was so unusually eager to get rid of the negro.

Among the stacks of wood around the stake driven firmly into the wet earth John saw there were piles of reeds. Which should have ensured that the flames would catch quickly. But the smoke and the slowness showed that much of the wood must still be green.

As soon as smoke began to ghost from the wood

around the feet of the black the noise began again. This time it was more ugly, more exultant.

John Ferris found himself torn. Wishing himself with a profound prayer that he could have been some other place. So that he need not watch this last scene of the tragedy. Yet, to watch and suffer was all that he could do. It might have been a hollow gesture, but there was nothing else that he could do.

Nothing.

It seemed an eternity before the flames began to burn with anything approaching earnest. Once Monk beckoned over Abe Mendoza, sending the tall man to the nearest of the cottages. Returning with a jug of fat that he threw on the fire, making it flare and smoke and spit. The mob cheered at that and John saw an old woman, wearing a shawl, come capering from the front of the crowd and do a little jig. It looked to him much like the woman who owned the house where he hid.

Brutus was writhing against his bonds, using all of his vast strength to try and tear himself free. As he watched his only friend dying, John wept. Salt tears trickling from the corners of his eyes, down his stubbled cheeks. And his nails dug so hard into his palms that tiny threads of blood burst through the skin.

Once, only once, did the black call out.

Then it was a tearing cry of agony and despair that soared above all other sounds, quieting the villagers for a moment.

'Lord, let me pass!!!'

As the flames rose, so John Ferris was able to make out more of the hideous details of his comrade's ending.

The face was seared and the eyes puffed shut. The skin peeled off the lips, which sank in until they revealed the whiteness of teeth. His clothes were quickly gone from him, revealing his magnificently muscled body. Also showing the women the nature of his endowal, which caused great merriment. The old woman that John had noticed before came out in front of the tortured man and lifted her skirt, cackling some piece of bawdy at the wretched black.

In the extremity of his suffering Brutus actually contrived to break one hand free of the chains, but the rest held him upright against the stake. More reeds were thrown on, and more wood, so that there were first higher flames, and then thicker smoke.

With his right hand Brutus beat at his own chest, shaking his head blindly to and fro, the hair all scorched away. John wept more at the sight, seeing that blood and water and fat streamed from the ends of the black's burned fingers.

Urged on by the good Christian folk around her, and by Monk and the gypsies, the crone in the shawl took one of the discarded flaming torches and hopped in and out, dodging the sparks and cinders, pressing the flaming end against the doomed negro's genitals, making him throw back his head and open his bleeding mouth in a soundless scream.

'She will die, Brutus. I swear that,' whispered John, shaking uncontrollably in the cold attic. He moved his feet, jumping as he knocked over a set of old fire-irons, including a heavy poker with a handle shaped like the head of a lion. Had there been anyone in the house they would certainly have heard the thunderous clatter and raised the alarm.

But he waited, pistol drawn and cocked. And nothing happened.

Once again he turned to the window. The snow was driving down with a greater sense of purpose now, making it hard to make out the details. If it persisted then the land would quickly begin to close down for the winter and any kind of journey would become nigh impossible.

The flames were higher, and the lower part of the negro's body was quite obscured. It seemed as if his legs had burned through, and his stomach must have been destroyed. From what Ferris had seen of other burnings, it was probable that the negro's bowels would have fallen away into the scorching fire.

Yet he lived.

That was the most horrific part of such a slaying. Often it seemed that a fire kept the victim alive for longer than would have appeared humanly possible, yet in the most cruel and appalling torment.

John had no idea of how long he had been watching the destruction of his friend, but it could not have been less than half of an hour.

And he still lived.

The blackened head moved feebly on the trunk and the stump of the one arm occasionally made a spasmodic flailing movement. Each time this happened the crowd cheered more vigorously, oblivious to the inclement weather that swooped all about them.

The end came suddenly.

There was a great plough-chain tight around the waist of what remained of Brutus York, and it was only that holding him upright as the flames roared, orange and yellow about him. Finally the lower part of his body was gone, and his chest and head toppled forwards into the raging inferno, and swiftly vanished from view.

At that there was a moan, almost of disappointment, from the mob, and then they fell silent, apart from a few scattered cheers. Some of them went to shake the hand of Robert Monk, including the woman with the shawl. The one that John Ferris had marked down for himself.

Gradually they dispersed and he watched them. Watching where Monk and the brothers went. Towards what seemed like an alehouse at the further end of the village high street. Only a few children were left around the smouldering, spitting embers of the execution fire, with the remains of Brutus York barely distinguishable among the glowing ashes. John saw the lady with the shawl over her head come scurrying through the whiteness feet leaving a trail in the fresh snow. He heard the back door of the house open and close with a resounding crash.

He stayed by the dormer window, his forehead pressed against the cold glass, staring blankly out into the swelling storm. Seeing the snow blanket the remnants of the great fire on the green. He tucked the pistol back in his belt and glanced around through the fast-fading light at the detritus in the attic. On an impulse he picked up the poker and hefted it, feeling the weight and the balance. It made a fair weapon.

'I swear I shall revenge you, Brutus. Revenge

against these . . . this pack of bastard animals.' His voice was harsh, strained, hurting his own throat. 'Forgive me, friend, that I let . . . I could do naught. I could not.' He was crying again. 'Forgive me, Brutus York. Friend.'

She was singing to herself. A pretty little song, and her voice was pleasant. Only cracking when she tried for a note that was too high or too long for her. The sound covered any noise that John might have made as he crept down the stairs, the poker gripped in his right hand. Stopping on each landing to listen and wait.

The door in the hall that led to the scullery was open and the singing continued. He could smell a stew bubbling on the stove in the kitchen. Food hadn't been that plentiful and he decided that if all went well he would take a few minutes out to fill his belly.

The clock still ticked its timeless way as he walked past it. Noticing that the hands stood at a few minutes before four in the afternoon.

The flags in the hall were scrubbed clean and he wondered whether there might be a brace of maids somewhere about. If there were, they would probably have gone with the others to the festivities.

Were it so, there was still the risk of their returning at any moment. With darkness beckoning and the weather so blighted, he would do well to press on with what he must do.

The old woman stood with her back to the hall, stirring a brown cauldron on the stove, humming to herself. The shawl was dripping water on the door that opened into the garden. Her hair was silver-grey, tied up at the nape of her neck.

At that moment she turned to meet him, her jaw dropping in shock. John saw that she was close to sixty, with apple-cheeks and blue eyes. A kindly face, that would have done well as someone running a dame school. He dragged back to his mind what he had seen from the attic.

The mocking. The torch jammed against the scorched body of his comrade and true friend.

'Who are . . .?' she began, fear darting to her eyes.

'I am the angel of vengeance, you bloody harridan,' he said, quietly.

The first blow felled her, knocking her semi-conscious to the stones, blood darkening them from the gaping wound at her temple.

The horror of it overcame him and a scarlet mist, filled with midnight shapes of raven black swept up over his mind. Helpless to aid Brutus in his lonely hour of dying, he could at least revenge him. The mist blotted out all reason and sense.

Only when he realised that the pounding was jarring his good arm did he stop hitting the corpse of the old woman with the poker.

What lay at his feet bore scant resemblance to a human being. The legs and body and arms were all there, the fingers clawed in the last moment of desperate agony. But there was nothing left above the neck. Nothing but a thick pulp. A crimson syrup that made him grue at its horror. Seeing the grey smears of brain among it, and the splintered shards of white bone, some with trailing hairs still adhering to them.

* * *

In a trim shed at the side of the house, close by the privy, John found several crocks of lamp oil. Before leaving on the next stage of his plans he poured several of them around the ground floor, splashing it about the corpse. Taking two more crocks with him as he went out into the evening, wincing at the cold and the driving snow.

Maxwell Green was quiet, apart from singing coming from the alehouse further down the road. That was certainly where Monk would be staying.

And that was where John Ferris, face set like winter marble, was going.

CHAPTER FIFTEEN

The insensate rage had slipped away from John, leaving him only with an iron reserve. Determined that the witchfinder should pay the ultimate price for his vicious cruelty. And if it was possible to also make the village pay for the way they had bayed at the passing of the negro . . . then that would be a savoury bonus.

He had pulled on his gloves, fearful of dropping the containers of oil. Picking his way along the track, rutted by carriages and carts. Wary, despite the sheeting snow that must surely keep everyone within doors. The wind came ripping into the hamlet from the nor'-east, along the line of cottages. On an impulse he suddenly saw a chance of a sweeter revenge, that might even aid him against Monk. A fire begun at one end might race along on the teeth of that wind, carried from dwelling to dwelling, igniting the thatch and wattle walls.

'A fine price,' he muttered, turning on his heel, moving into the wind, crouching against its ferocity.

Providence smiled on him. The last building at the eastern end of Maxwell Green was a tumbledown barn, packed with dry straw and with more canisters of lamp-oil stored on shelves.

Everything that a man could seek to begin an inferno that would tear the malign heart from Maxwell Green.

The only concern he felt was that some man or woman might see the fire before it was well enough established. But those in their cottages were not going to sally out into the blizzard. And those in the alehouse were having too good a time to even poke their noses beyond the doors.

He crouched in the barn, gathering the straw against the wall of the building next door. Soaking oil around, splashing it high on the straw, on the ground, and against daubed walls. Carefully using his flint and tinder-box to start the delicate, pale flames. Blowing on them to give them strength. Watching as they spread, feeding on the oil and straw. Gaining power and ferocity.

Only when he was satisfied that the fire was well established did John move out. Keeping in the centre of the lane where nobody might recognise him. Looking behind him for the first signs that his arson was working, but the snow muffled all.

The alehouse was noisy, filled with bellows of drunken laughter and chanting. The rooms at the front were lit, but curtains were pulled across them and he could make out nothing behind them. Yet he guessed that it would be there that Monk was holding court. With the slattern, Hall, and the two surviving brothers.

'Mary?' he questioned.

The snow eased for a few minutes, and John was finally able to see what he'd hoped. With the pond frozen over and half of the men well-drunk the fire was going to prove a total conqueror. With nobody able to stand against it. The buildings were so tightly packed on that side of the street that flames were already leaping from roof to roof, igniting the eaves and thatch.

He remembered the large building with the dead woman in its scullery, and ran back to it. Again carefully lighting the oil. Breaking up three chairs, and tearing down sheets from the beds. Piling it up and watching with a bitter satisfaction as the flames began to roar.

When he went back into the street, Ferris stopped a moment, hesitating. The fire on the far side was already raging so fiercely that it was turning evening into noon, the wind tearing the flames into great orange and yellow streamers. The village was like an ants' nest after a careless heel has broken into it. Boiling with people, all running and yelling, hither and thither. Calling for help for some trapped, urging others to flee their dwellings while there was yet time.

None of that meant much to John, whose eyes were set on the alehouse.

A first-floor window was open and he saw a man leaning from it, a woman behind him, silhouetted against the light. It was the witchfinder.

John drew his pistol, tugging back on the miquelet lock, taking careful aim at Monk. His one desire had been to make the villain suffer, eye to eye. Now all he wanted was his death.

He was less than thirty paces away, at the angle of a grocer's shop opposite, near the stables. Finger on the trigger, drawing a careful bead on the man's throat. Finger tightening . . .

The thrown dagger missed him by a bare finger's breadth, thudding into a heavy beam, blade vibrating with the force. He spun round, coming within an ace of putting the ball through the head of a six-year-old girl standing staring at him, sucking her thumb.

Beyond her, half-turned to run, was . . .

'Abe Mendoza . . .'

The tall man shook an angry fist at him, ducking away round the back of one of the small houses, sidling away and going right. Towards the fires.

The head at the window was withdrawn and John heard the crash of a shutter slamming shut. Once again Robert Monk had escaped him by a whisker. But if anything was to be remedied from the situation then he might as well pursue the gipsy. The way he felt at that moment, any death would be more satisfying than no death at all.

Despite the hopelessness of their task, against a wind that had risen to a screaming gale, the villagers were still trying to save their houses and homes. Forming a chain and passing leather buckets brimming with icy water and hurling it desperately against the flames that now engulfed a third of the street. The fire seemed to welcome their efforts, hissing and steaming, but raging utterly unabated.

Mendoza stopped twice, turning to look at his pursuer. John Ferris closed remorselessly, running light-footed through the slush and ice, keeping the pistol cocked in his right hand.

Then the gipsy disappeared.

Cutting to his right, vanishing behind a wall of driven snow, mingled with choking smoke. But John glimpsed his move, pressing closer behind him.

The house where John had murdered the old woman was also blazing well, and the gipsy headed towards it, going around the side, silhouetted against the bright flames.

Ferris burst into the back garden, halting when he realised that Mendoza must have hidden. Somewhere very close. There were only the trees, and a trim hen-house, with a slatted front. A neatly-carpentered door.

That stood open an inch or two.

John moved cautiously closer. Though Abraham might have thrown one of his knives, it was likely that he had at least one more hid about him.

'Come out, you bastard gippo,' John called to the hiding man. Nothing happened. No movement in the shadowed hut.

'I will put a ball through you where you skulk.'

'I didn't kill the black. Didn't take him. That was Danny. Not me, squire.'

'Out.'

The door swung open and Abraham Mendoza crawled out, a pitiful sight. His long coat flapped about his ankles and it was smeared with mud and chicken-droppings. The house behind him was blazing well, great tongues of fire even coming through the doors that covered the cellar steps. Doubtless where oil had dripped down into the basement and ignited in the blackness.

'Stand, and keep your hands out where I can watch them.'

'I have no weapon, Captain Ferris. None.'

'Liar.'

The gipsy shook his head. The long black curls were ringing wet, dotted now with odd flakes of snow. He was turning and staring about him, seeking some way out.

'Don't kill me, Captain."

'Why not?'

'Because . . . Because Danny'll shoot you if you do!' flinging out a hand to point towards the house.

If John Ferris had not already been standing with finger tight on the trigger of the Ripoll pistol, he might have died for the ruse.

Mendoza was ambidextrous. Throwing a second knife at John with his left hand, that had been partly concealed behind his back. John was able to duck it, his attention diverted for a second by the old trick. But he might not have been able to save himself from the yelling man as he came lunging in with a third knife, narrow-bladed like an Italian stiletto, in his right hand.

The pulling of the trigger was the instinct of a soldier.

The aiming at the stomach of the gipsy was simple skill, the product of long hours of practice with the heavy gun.

Mendoza folded over like a fawning courtier, dropping his knife, falling to his kness with a moan of pain.

'Fuck you . . . Fuck . . . Killed me, you bugger. Killed me . . .

'Not yet.' Smoke billowed from the house making him blink, coughing. 'Not yet, but soon, Stand.'

'I am dead.'

'No.'

'Spare me, Captain. I can give you Monk and all if you . . .'

'I will have him. Stand.'

Painfully, menaced by John's sword, the gipsy hauled himself erect, hands clasped over his belly, blood leaking over his thighs.

John had seen such wounds, confident that Mendoza was as good as dead. The ball was lodged deep in his intestines and there was scant chance of survival. Much as he would have liked the villainous killer to have suffered a long and lingering death he wished even more to see the man die.

He stepped closer, thrusting with the tip of the sword at Abraham's face, making him move back. A couple of paces nearer to the fire. The doors to the cellar, flames and smoke streaking orange from between them, were less than five yards behind.

'Mercy.'

John flashed the sword again, sending the gipsy two more steps backwards. 'Mercy! The very word should blast your tongue! There is no mercy in such a cold-hearted rogue as you. You show none. You shall receive none.'

Another move, this time opening up a deep, slicing cut along the angle of Mendoza's jaw, under the curling beard. Forcing him to the very brink of the doors. The gipsy glanced behind himself, feeling the intense heat. Seeing then the death that John Ferris planned for him. Opening his mouth to scream.

'No,' yelled John. 'For Brutus!!'

Striking at him, the sword sinking several inches deep into the man's right shoulder. The impact sending him toppling back on top of the doors. That opened under him and he vanished with a shrill cry of terror, flames billowing out into the snow-filled air.

John Ferris stood, panting with the exertion, looking down into the pit of fire. Seeing the gypsy wallowing about, struggling to his feet. Trying to jump, fingers scrabbling at the edge of the drop. Reaching it. Fighting to pull himself up. John looked down, stone-hearted. Seeing the man's clothes burning from his body in strips of flame. The hair frizzling and smoking. Skin peeling.

'For Brutus,' he said, quietly, and kicked at the fingers, sending Mendoza back once more into the inferno of the cellar.

This time the gipsy disappeared and did not come back. There was something that blundered about for a moment or two, mewing like a drowning kitten. Then it was still, the only sound the crackle of the flames.

The air was filled with the stench of roasting meat.

It was with the greatest reluctance that John Ferris decided he must leave the village. The whole of Maxwell Green seemed to have caught fire in the rising wind, snow dashing against the flames. It would never bring back poor, tortured Brutus York, but at least the negro went to eternity with a fine funeral pyre. And the community paid a price for their cruelty.

On the hopeful chance of seeing Monk near the ale-house, John reloaded his pistol and walked around the outskirts of the hamlet, coming up behind the tavern. It was now firmly and irrevocably fixed in his mind that he would kill the last brother and the slattern, Hall, along with the witchfinder himself. It was a deed that needed to be done. It was his duty to purge the earth of such vile evil.

Even his feelings for Mary had been overpowered by his hatred for Monk. He knew that his betrothed lady would come back to him as soon as she was freed.

The back of the tavern was in darkness, but for a single casement that opened just above his head. John was frozen into stillness, fearing that it might be the witchfinder himself. A head came out, peering at the snow.

Suddenly seeing him in the shadows.

'Who is . . .? John? John Ferris, is that you?'

It was her.

His heart's desire. His only true love. The finest wench that drew breath.

'Mary, it is I.'

'Are you alone?'

Her voice was strained, tense.

'I am.'

'Have you seen aught of Abe Mendoza?'

'I have sent him to be with his brother.'

'Where?'

'In Hell, with the damned.'

'Killed!'

'Aye. But enow of this talk. Come with me, my sweet Mary. There are two horses in the woods. One belonged to poor Brutus York."

'The black! You saw that?'

'Aye. Quickly and we can be away.'

Snow drove into his face, blinding him for a moment, and, when he looked up, Mary Viller had gone. He thought that she must be on her way down to the rear of the alehouse to join him and his heart leaped within his breast.

But, she came back.

'Mary, make haste.'

'You fool!' There was a mix of anger and contempt in her voice.

'I did . . .' he stammered, shocked then into silence.

'Think you that I was not with Robert of my own free will?"

'I thought he held you 'gainst . . .'

'While you have tracked the length and breadth of the land I have laid him in warm beds. His lips upon my breasts, his member deep within me. He has fucked me where you would not, John.'

'But my parents. The silver.'

'Fool, fool, damned fool!!' She laughed at his dismay. 'I see your great white face, goggling at me, Johnny. Your parents were witches. I betrayed the silver. I saw you that day Robert laid his snare for you and I told them of your coming. I have loved being with him and will stay with him.'

'No!'

'Aye. bonny laddy. Aye.' Mocking him. 'I

warned him the black would come one day and he put words about, spiced with a little gold.'

'I do not believe you.' But his tone betrayed the truth. His heart felt empty, filled with ice. This was what he had given near a twelve-month of his life for. For this.

For nothing.

'Go, and never return.'

'I shall slay Monk and the others for what they have done.'

'I have done you greater ill, you booby. Will you slay me, you fumbling cuckold?'

Had she been within reach, he would have killed her on the spot. Ripped her face from the skull with his bare hands.

'I have told Robert. Sent him word, Johnny. He will be here to take you with the help of this village. They will love you not for this fire, Johnny.'

'Mary . . .'

'Yes, my sweet dove . . .' she teased. But there was a note of hatred in the mocking voice.

'When next I come to seek that bastard Monk, I shall slay him. And the third of the gippo brood. And that foul whore Liza Hall.'

'Lest they slay you first.'

'Aye, truly said. And now I know what part you have played in my misfortunes this last year, Mary . . .' He paused. 'Also, I shall kill you.'

'So much for love . . .' but he could catch a new note in her voice. Fear.

'You have my oath upon it, mistress.'

'Then this is the end of our fine beginning, Johnny. Fare thee well.'

'No, bitch. I wish that you might rot in Hades

with the rest. No end to a beginning. All that is water 'neath the bridges. For us, Mary, it is the beginning of the end.'

John turned upon his heel and vanished into the driving snow. The woman watched after him for a long while. Then closed the casement and locked it.

THUS ENDS BOOK TWO OF THE WITCHES.

WHAT MICHELLE REMEMBERS YOU WILL NEVER FORGET . . .

MICHELLE REMEMBERS

by MICHELLE SMITH & DR LAWRENCE PAZDER

The horrific true story of a five-year-old child surrendered to the devil. Only now, with the aid of Dr Lawrence Pazder, is Michelle Smith able to relive the terrifying ordeal which she suffered at the hands of a group of Satanists. An ordeal which turned into an extraordinary battle between innocence and evil for the soul of a five-year-old child . . .

AUTOBIOGRAPHY 0 7221 7958 8 £1.75

THEY'LL GIVE THEIR ALL FOR A PIECE OF PARADISE . . .

California Dreamers

Norman Bogner

Rodeo Drive is Los Angeles' priciest square mile, where the well-heeled hedonists of fantasy city spend their millions. To this Mecca of merchandising are drawn the beautiful, the bizarre, the all-consumingly ambitious:

BOBBY the idealistic architect who longed to build churches – and instead created citadels for the worship of wealth...

CLAIRE the jilted small-town beauty who followed him West – to success in a business where only the most ruthless survive...

HILLARY too young, too voluptuous, too rich – she snatched any thrills she could get, and paid the price...

GIOVANNI ex-movie actor and society restaurant owner – who had laid-back LA at his feet until he found he cared for someone...

Where money talks – and walks, and makes love – they'll sell body and soul to buy a dream of paradise . . .

GENERAL FICTION **0 7221 17604** **£1.75**

LITTLE GIRLS LOST

Doris Shannon

'Grasping the ashtray in moist hands, Erin waited. Sally was quiet now. The only sound was her own laboured breathing. Now she could hear the thud of the crazed woman's feet as she approached the room. Erin tensed and waited for the door to open. As it swung back she raised the ashtray, holding it in both hands. She allowed Andromeda to take two steps into the room before she crashed it down. At the last second the woman seemed to scent danger and she moved to one side.
The woman gave a throaty chuckle. Hands closed around Erin's throat and tightened. She clawed at the hands. Coloured dots swam in front of her eyes. I'm dying, she thought. The pressure slackened and she gasped for breath. Then she screamed as the whip cut across her raw back. It came down again and again. She tried to crawl away, but the whip cut across her thighs, her legs. She shrieked in agony . . .'

Sheltered all her life, Erin would never have believed what her first visit to her godmother would lead to. But when three girls go missing and her godmother is asked to investigate their disappearance, Erin finds herself the bait for a potentially lethal trap . . .

HORROR 0 7221 7736 4 £1.95